tara

THE QUEST FOR THE
SHYN
EMERALDS

Hi Arush
Congrats n have fun
Usha n Mukund

Roopa Pai suspects she has alien blood, for two reasons. One, she loved history in school. And two, although an adult, she mostly reads children's books.

Roopa has won a Children's Book Trust award for science writing. Among her published works are a four-book science series, *Sister Sister* (Pratham Books), and two girl-power books, *Kaliyuga Sita* and *Mechanic Mumtaz* (UNICEF).

When she is not dreaming up plots for her stories, she goes on long solo bicycle rides, and takes children on history and nature walks in Bangalore. You can find her at *www.roopapai.in*.

taranauts

BOOK ONE

THE QUEST FOR THE SHYN EMERALDS

Roopa Pai

Illustrated by Priya Kuriyan

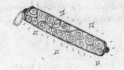

hachette
INDIA

First published in 2009 by Hachette India

www.hachetteindia.com

This edition copyright © Hachette India 2009
Text copyright © Roopa Pai 2009
Illustrations copyright © Priya Kuriyan 2009

10 9 8 7 6 5 4 3

ISBN: 978-93-80143-51-4

Hachette Book Publishing India Pvt. Ltd
4th/5th Floors, Corporate Centre,
Sector 44, Gurgaon 122003, India

Typset in Perpetua 13.5/16 by
Eleven Arts, New Delhi

Printed in India by
Manipal Technologies Ltd, Manipal

For Chetu and Ronu,
Tarasuns of my universe

TARA
Magmacup
MegaStage
Zum Skar
Glo
Dazl
Syntilla
Magmalift

Mithya

Ever dreamed about *falling off the map*? About tumbling through a rabbit hole into a *whole different dimension*? About visiting a *brand new universe*? Well, guess what? *now you can!*

Whoaaaaa! Hang on a minute. There are things about the New Universe (it's called Mithya, by the way) that will be different and unfamiliar, so here's a handy guide. You may read it now, or you may go straight to page 12, and come back and look stuff up whenever you need to. Here goes!

EARTH	MITHYA
One somewhat spherical blue-green planet. . .	An entire universe, with eight somewhat spherical 'worlds' (Dazl, Glo, Shyn, Shimr, Lustr, Sparkl, Syntilla, Glytr) . . .
. . .that wobbles around in space. . .	. . . that bob in an endless sea called Dariya, around an ill-tempered volcano called Kay Laas . . .

EARTH	MITHYA

. . . in the light of a big golden star called the sun.

. . . in the light of a superstar sun called Tara, made up of 32 'stars'—the Tarasuns—of different colours. Each world has four 'stars' of a particular colour shining down on it—emerald green, amethyst purple, ruby red, sapphire blue . . .

The earth rotates around its own axis each earth day, each part facing the sun for half the time (day) and facing away for the other half (night).

The worlds flip over into the sea once a Taraday (called octite) all at the same time. They all face Tara for two-thirds the time (Taralite) and face away for the other one-third (Taranite)

An earth day has 24 hours—12 hours of day and 12 of night. Each hour is divided into 60 minutes.

An octite has 48 dings— 32 dings of Taralite and 16 of Taranite. Each ding is divided into 64 dinglings.

Earth day roughly runs from 6 a.m. to 6 p.m., and earth night from 6 p.m. to midnight, and then again from midnight to 6 a.m.

Taralite runs from 1 o'ding to 32 o'ding, and Taranite from 32 o'ding to 48 o'ding.

EARTH	MITHYA
7 earth days make a week. 4 weeks make a month. 12 months make a year.	8 octites make an octoll. 16 octolls make an octet. 4 octets make an octon.
Earth people are called human beings (by us).	Mithya people are called mithyakos. Little mithyakos are called mithyakins.
Humans live all over the earth, except at the cold, cold North and South Poles.	Most mithyakos live on the Upsides, the halves that stay out of the water for 32 dings each Taraday. Downsides are scary, unexplored places, full of creatures of the darkness, and also the not-so-nice mithyakos that are not accepted on the Upsides.
Earth has no single Absolute Ruler.	Mithya does—the wise, brave, benevolent Emperaza, Shoon Ya. He lives on the top of Kay Laas, in the Land of Eternal Taralite, the Land of Nevernite. Each world of Mithya has its own ruler, who is either a Maraza or a Marani.

11

EARTH	MITHYA
Human beings can be nice, wicked, generous, greedy, caring, cruel, smart, dumb, fun, boring, and everything in between.	Mithyakos can be nice, wicked, generous, greedy, caring, cruel, smart, dumb, fun, boring, and everything in between.

All okay so far? One word of warning, though. Sure it all looks pretty and peaceful, but don't be fooled. In the fiery lands under the heaving, writhing seabed of Dariya, is Mithya's *ultimate* maximum security prison, guarded by the water spirits, Here, you will find Shoon Ya's evil twin, the fearsome demon Shaap Azur, just as powerful as Shoon Ya, but *all bad*.

So far, Shoon Ya has been able to keep him in chains, and the mithyakos are safe, but how much longer can the peace last? All it will take is one careless water spirit, and Shaap Azur could escape, bursting through the heaving seabed of Dariya and screaming *revenge*!

But don't let *that* worry you right now. If you're all set, fasten your seat belts, hold on to your map, and *awayyyyyy you go*!

one

'Ma,' shouted Zvala, already beginning to turn red and hot as she always did when she was stressed. 'We are getting really, really late for the Supertaranova celebrations! You know how special it is—it happens only on an Octoversary, and today is the first Octoversary on Mithya *since I was born!*'

'We have plenty of time, puchkin, and Shyn is not that far from Kay Laas, you know,' said her mother calmly, fixing Zvala glittering purple pins into her hair and spritzing her with something out of a shiny blue bottle.

'What new product are you trying this time, Ma? You know nothing really works to cool me down . . .'

'Doesn't mean I should stop trying!' said Ma. 'I do want to be able to cuddle my little mithyakin when she's upset, but I can never do it because she gets too hot!'

'Oh, Ma! I'm not a little mithyakin anymore! I'm eight octons old!' Zvala squirmed out of Ma's hug and peeked at the mirror. Her skin had returned to its normal colour. She tossed her long, thick, black hair and smiled. 'Now that's more like pretty me again . . .'

Ma rolled her eyes, picked up her bag and gently pushed Zvala through the door. 'Ah, here comes the aquauto I booked. Let's go.'

'The Kay Laas Magmalift, please,' said Ma to the driver, 'At zipspeed.'

The aquauto sped to the Magnarail station and got in line with the rest of the aquautos heading for the magnetic tracks. Once on the tracks, it pulled in its wheels, hovered uncertainly for a dingling, and then zoomed away towards the port at a terrific speed.

Before Zvala knew it, the aquauto had reached the Port of Shyn, and was skimming furiously over the clear waters of Dariya, towards Kay Laas.

'Eeeeeeee! We're flying over the sea!' screamed Zvala excitedly. 'But I can hardly see the surface of the water—there must be a *trizillion* aquautos here today!'

'Well, who would want to miss out on the celebrations?' said Ma. 'You know that all mithyakos love Shoon Ya. And today is not just any old anniversary of him becoming Emperaza; it is the Octoversary—he has ruled us for eight octons and we have had only peace and happiness in all that time.'

'I know. I too think Shoon Ya is an absolute rock star. But tell me something—why is an *eighth* anniversary or birthday such a big deal, anyway?'

'Well,' said Ma. 'Eight is a very important number in Mithya. We have eight worlds, for one thing—remember their names from your Mithyography lessons?'

Uh-oh. Zvala knew Shyn, of course—it was her world, the northern world, and she knew of Glo, in the west, where her all-time favouritest pop star Dana Suntana was from—but who could remember what the other worlds were?

'Ma,' she said quickly. 'We're almost there!'

'You're right, let's start getting our things together,' said Ma, forgetting the Mithyography question.

Zvala heaved a sigh of relief. 'Note to self,' she mumbled under her breath. 'Keep. Your. Big. Mouth. Shut.'

'Zarpa! ZARPAAAA! You are in *such* trouble! Let me get my hands on you this time . . . You know I've *got* to get to the Supertaranova in time or the Marani will be mad at me. . .'

Oops, late again! Zarpa shut off Papa's angry voice on the summoner she always wore around her neck. Sometimes she wished she was just a normal mithyakin who didn't have to carry the annoying thing. But Papa was high up in the government of Sparkl, the eastern world, and all government officials and their families had to carry summoners by law.

It was her Mulkum class that was to blame, of course. Zarpa was so good at twisting her body into all kinds of fantastic postures on the Mulkum pole, and enjoyed it so much, that her schoolmates were always begging her to stay back and help them. But she really *should* have remembered that today was her dad's big day.

Zarpa sneaked a guilty look at her dingdial as she ran. It was 27 o'ding, already—and the Supertaranova was due to start at half-past 28. The aqualimo from the Marani's palace would be waiting.

She had to quickly change out of her sweaty clothes, dress in something that made her look *really* uncool— Uffpah! How she *hated* wearing stupid spangled dresses, but she would have to, today—and hope they made it in time for the 28 o'ding Magmalift.

Just now, she was moving at zipspeed, which meant she was zigging and zagging and sort of sliding along the ground rather than actually running. She wasn't sure how she did that, and she was careful not to do it in front of her friends because they teased her, but now, getting back quickly was the important thing.

'Pssst! Come in here, quickly!' Mama was holding open the back door. Zarpa flashed her a grateful smile as she ran straight into the shower. Her clothes were all laid out on the bed when she came out—Yay! Mama had chosen the least frilly, lacy thing she owned.

Zarpa brushed her short spiky hair down vigorously and laced up her emerald green sneakers. In five dinglings flat, she was ready to go.

'Pappy!' she called gaily, winking at Mama. 'Zarpy's all sssset!'

Papa came storming in. 'Wha..? How? Where were you . . . ?'

There was a pause as he looked at the cheeky face grinning up at him. Zarpa could see he was really making an effort to look angry. Then he threw back his head and laughed.

'Come here, you rascal!' he said, scooping her up in his arms. 'I know you and your Mama have been up to something here. Let's go, now.'

'Zarpaaa!' groaned Mama, noticing her sneakers for the first time. 'Sneakers? With that dress? You are not going to any party in those!'

'Let her be, Mama,' said Papa. 'She looks fabulous. Bet no one in Mithya has as pretty a mithyakin as mine!'

'*Sssssseeee?!*' Zarpa jumped into the aqualimo, pulling Mama in with her. Papa squeezed in beside the driver, and they were off.

Tufan hung back a little from the rest of his noisy, boisterous class. He had sneaked in two of his smallest pets on the school trip—Squik, his furry gileli with the sharp teeth and the waffling nose, who loved to snuggle in warm, dark places, and Chik-Chik, his stripy, inquisitive kipchali with the power to grow back any limb it lost. And he didn't want anyone to find out.

He knew what would happen then—the girls would shriek and try to climb the walls, and the boys would grab the little guys and pull their tails. He would get all mad and begin to breathe really hard, and suddenly, his classmates would be flying all over the place, banging into walls, crashing through windows, zooming backwards into who-knows-what.

Then of course, Ms Kha Doos would arrive to see what the noise was about, and Tufan would be marched off to the headmaster's office. The headmaster would write a polite letter to Azza and Azzi saying that he showed a 'strong resistance to discipline, and disrespect for authority, and exhibited violent tendencies', and would advise them to find another school more suitable for 'a boy of his temperament'.

Azzi would cry and say she didn't know how to bring up a motherless child, Azza would not talk to him for several octites, and everyone, except his beloved big brother Dada, would wonder why he couldn't be just a little more like Dada.

Not that all the drama made much of a difference to Tufan. It had happened so many times. What mattered was that through all that, Dada loved him. Plus, he really did not know why strange things happened to people and things around him when he got mad.

It wasn't something he could control, really.

But he didn't want to be sent home before the end of this particular school trip. His school had been invited to the Octoversary! It was the first time in his nine-octon-old life that he would be stepping out of the southern world of Lustr! He wasn't going to miss it for anything!

'Lustr Secondary!' Ms Kha Doos's voice came booming over the megaphone. 'To the big yellow hoverbuses! Now!'

They were off! As he quietly fed Squik and Chik-Chik their favourite juicy purple zamunberries, Tufan's eyes were glued to the see-through floors of the hoverbuses.

Oh, Dariya was beautiful. Dazzling meenmaach swam in the clear waters, swishing their tails this way and that, their glittering fins a rainbow of colour. Mean-looking muggars, still as rocks, smiled toothily up at him, ready to strike like lightning if he made one false move. Seasliths, their bodies long, lithe and fluorescent, flashed like quicksilver and were gone before he could identify them.

As they sped along, Tufan could feel something strange happening to him. He was feeling, well . . . *heavier*. Quickly, he looked at his arms and legs. Had he gotten fatter all of a sudden? No, it didn't look like it. But with every dingling, he was certainly growing much heavier.

'I hope this doesn't get me sent back home now,' he said to himself, worriedly, as he felt his weight go up by another couple of tols. 'Uffpah, I hope I can still walk when I get off the hoverbus . . .'

'The Magmalift!' shouted Ms Kha Doos. 'Move it. Now!'

Tufan stood up and began to walk slowly and awkwardly to the door of the hoverbus.

Two

Ma held Zvala's hand tightly as they joined the sea of mithyakos heading towards the giant Magmalifts inside Kay Laas.

Inside, it was unbelievably noisy. There was a huge bunch of students in Lustr Secondary T-shirts chattering at the tops of their voices. From somewhere below came a constant deep rumbling. The Magmalift wobbled a little. Zvala clutched Ma's hand nervously.

'What's happening, Ma?'

she shouted brightly. If she was scared, she wasn't going to let on.

But Ma didn't hear her. Zvala tried again, a little more loudly. 'Ma, what's happening?'

'Whoa! Sssstop sssscreaming in my ear!' A girl about her own age was squeezed up against Zvala, and she looked very annoyed.

'Oops! I'm sorry!' said Zvala, her voice trembling a little. 'I didn't realize . . .'

The girl's face cracked into a smile, and Zvala felt herself smiling back instantly.

'Is it your first time in the Magmalift?' the girl asked Zvala.

Zvala nodded.

'Sssee, basically,' said the girl, with a little lisp. 'There's all this magma—liquid rock and metal—deep under the ocean. Once a ding, it comes bursting out of the blowhole at the top of Kay Laasss. When it does, it takes the Magmalift with it. You may feel a bit odd the first time, but it helps if you . . .'

But Zvala heard nothing else. The deep rumbling turned into a deafening roar. The Magmalift stood stock still for a long moment and then, suddenly, zoomed upward at such speed that Ma's hand was torn out of Zvala's. Her cheeks were pulled downward, and her body felt unbearably heavy. Strong forces pushed her against the wall of the Magmalift and pinned her there. Her ears popped shut. Her stomach turned a couple of trizillion somersaults.

Suddenly, Zvala felt something run up her leg. Her mouth opened in a silent scream. She hated creepy-crawlies at the best of times, and this one seemed furry, too!

Just when she thought her head, or her heart, or both, must burst, the Magmalift exploded out of the blowhole with a thunderous sound, and then floated gently down in a soft bouncy landing. The red-hot magma was pulled into the ginormous magmacups by strong magmatational forces and sent swiftly downwards into the recycling chambers under the ocean.

The doors opened, and everyone started filing out. But Zvala stood transfixed, unable to move. She could feel the 'thing' on her leg! She felt herself turning a bright, glowing red, and getting hotter and hotter.

Suddenly the 'thing' gave a startled squeak and jumped off, straight into the open palms of a tall boy who was looking at her very accusingly. 'You scared him—you scared my little gileli!' he spat.

Zvala was so startled by the unfairness of the accusation and so relieved that the 'thing' was gone that she could only open and close her mouth like a meenmaach.

'Hey, leave her alone!' It was the spiky-haired girl again.

She turned to the gileli. 'C'mere, you little fuzzy-buzzy, you!' she crooned softly. The gileli jumped into her cupped palms. A kipchali peeked out of the boy's right pocket.

'Hellloooo, who have we here *now*?' said the girl, putting the gileli in her pocket and extending her palms again. The kipchali jumped right in.

The boy looked stunned. 'They've never done that before,' he said wonderingly.

Zvala opened one eye cautiously and looked. 'Zarpa,' said the girl, returning the animals and offering her hand. 'Tufan,' said the boy, stretching out his hand slowly, as if it weighed a hundred tols. They were both looking at her.

'I'm Zvala,' she said.

'You're very red,' said Tufan.

Zvala felt herself grow redder—and hotter. 'And you,' she said, 'are the rudest boy I've ever met.'

For some reason, both Zarpa and Tufan found that hilarious. Tufan began to laugh, and water came squirting out of him. It came out in sprays from his hands, his arms, his chest, and his legs.

Now it was Tufan's turn to look confused. Zvala and Zarpa were hooting with laughter.

Suddenly, Zvala stopped. 'Hey, guess what? That water

really cooled me down. Usually it takes me a long, long time to cool down completely when I am super tense, and nothing has ever worked before. How do you do that?'

'You know what,' said Tufan slowly. 'I have absolutely no idea.'

'Tufan!' boomed Ms Kha Doos. 'Out of the Magmalift! This instant!'

Tufan ran, waving a quick bye.

'Whoops! I've got to go too,' said Zarpa. 'My parents are waiting outside. See you around.' Zvala looked out, found Ma in the crowd, and stepped out of the Magmalift.

It was the brightest, sparkliest, funnest party Zarpa had ever seen.

All around her, as far as the eye could see, were blue lawns bursting with flowers. Mithyakos were everywhere—laughing, dancing in groups, greeting friends, taking rides on the Blowhole Hop-On-Hop-Off tourist buses, and eating and eating and eating. Mithyakins ran around, biting off sweet sticky fluffs of cloud candy in eight different flavours and grabbing the sparkly balloons that floated right above their heads.

There were giant wheels and merry-go-rounds, trampolines and moon-walkers, a gigantic wave pool and water slides, hair-braiding stations and robopuppet shows, nail-art kiosks and tattoo artists, hovercarpet rides and slipperypole slides.

On several stages in the party area, musicians, dancers,

25

magicians, gymnasts and acrobats performed to happy crowds. A huge shiny emerald tent with purple stars all over it turned out to be a giant wardrobe, full of cute berets and cowboy hats, glittery belts and fancy sandals, spangled dresses with fairy wings, giant hoop earrings and beaded bracelets in every colour, and the most darling clutch bags.

And you could pick up anything from there for free—and take it home!

Zvala had just picked up bright orange hoops to go with her new orange pants and was reaching for a silver bandanna when she heard the announcement over the speakers—'And now, mithyakos, coming up on MegaStage in just a few dinglings . . . SUPERTARANOVA!'

'Eeeeeeeee!' screeched Zvala. 'Ma, see you at MegaStage!' And she was gone.

Zvala did not stop running until she finally saw the entrance to MegaStage, stopping only for a quick glance at the seating plan. Each world had a separate area, with the VIM—Very Important Mithyakos—of that world sitting up in front in the reserved seats. Behind them, it was free seating—whoever got there first grabbed the best places.

Squeezing her way through people's legs and sometimes crawling on all fours, she reached the first few rows of the Shyn Area, and started making her 'poor me' face at everyone around. In a dingling, Shynkos in the first row had moved up to let her squeeze in.

And not a moment too soon—the show was about to begin!

There was a fanfare of crescent horns and conches. Riding his favourite shardula and laden with seasliths, which had wound themselves into fluorescent garlands around his head, arms and neck, came Emperaza Shoon Ya, dark curly locks flowing down his broad back, black eyes snapping fire.

When he smiled, his teeth glittered just as brightly as the diamonds in his ears. Around his waist was tied a length of gold astersilk shot through with all the colours of the stars of Tara—emerald green, sapphire blue, ruby red, amethyst purple, citrine yellow, coral pink, turquoise blue-green, and silvery white.

Behind him, riding her makara, came Shuk Tee, Shoon Ya's most dependable deputy and the Most Intelligent Being in

Mithya, fiercely and absolutely loyal to Shoon Ya. It was whispered among the mithyakos that Shoon Ya never took a decision without first discussing it with her. Very few mithyakos had ever seen her—she never left Kay Laas.

Today, Shuk Tee was dressed in dazzling white, as she always was in times of peace. In times of war or crisis, Shuk Tee, it was said, dressed in bloodcurdling red, and struck terror into the hearts of the enemies of Mithya.

Shoon Ya rode to the centre of the stage. Dismounting, he walked regally to the front of the stage and raised his staff for silence.

'Good People of Mithya,' he boomed, 'Welcome to Kay Laas! Thank you all for coming to take part in the Octoversary. You are all very fortunate—for the first time in eight octons, our benevolent guardians, the 32 Tarasuns, have descended from the sky onto Kay Laas to put on a fabulous show for us. They will be here for ten dinglings, after which they have to hurry back to their places in the sky so that they can continue to bless us with their warmth and glorious light. Ten dinglings only, mithyakos, so feast your eyes.

'LET . . . THE CELEBRATIONS . . . BEGIN!'

There was a thunderous roar of applause, cheering, hoots and whistles. The Kay Laas brass band struck up a merry tune. Onto the stage danced the 32 Tarasuns, in eight colour-coded groups of four stars each.

Escorting them on stage were the rulers of each of the eight worlds—the Maraza of Dazl brought the Corals, the Marani of Glo the Rubies, the Maraza of Chimr the

Citrines, the Marani of Shyn the Emeralds, the Maraza of Syntilla the Silvers, the Marani of Sparkl the Amethysts, the Maraza of Glytr the Turquoises, and finally, the Marani of Lustr the Sapphires.

Zvala clapped the loudest for the Shyn Emeralds, and almost as loud for the Glo Rubies—hey, they were the ones who kept Dana Suntana warm and happy, after all!

The Tarasuns cheered Shoon Ya. He bowed in return, then came down from the stage to take his place on the Crystal Throne in the centre of the first row. Shuk Tee took her place on his right, and the Marazas and Maranis arranged themselves on either side of them. Zvala saw Ma looking for her, and waved her over.

The violins struck a merry tune, and the Tarasuns began to dance. They twirled and swirled in beautiful patterns of light, they cartwheeled and spun and came together in starry waves and chains, they shone their radiant light into the darkest spaces and left trails of sparkling Taradust behind them as they flew over the mithyakos.

Everyone cheered, their faces shining, their skins aglow, their smiles warm and happy. Zvala squeezed Ma's hand excitedly. She was so glad she had come.

KAAAA-BLOOOM!

The explosion rocked Megastage from side to side, sweeping the Tarasuns into the wings. Dust flew in every direction, and icy evil-smelling smoke swirled around the mithyakos, blotting out the light. Black soot settled on shining skins.

Everyone screamed.

A huge, hairy creature had burst through the centre of the stage. His long hair was matted, and his beard was long and knotty. His teeth were long and yellow as a wilderwolf's fangs, and the corner of his mouth drooled spittle. He wore a dirty, ill-fitting robe of sackcloth that had been darned and patched many times over. His tiny, mean eyes swept the room, and his glacier breath turned the mithyakos' blood to ice.

'We are done for!' moaned the Shynkos next to Zvala, holding her head in her hands.

'It's Shaap Azur! He is free!'

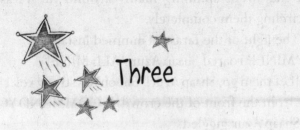

Three

'**G**RRRRRROOOAAARRRGHHHH!'
Shaap Azur's roar shattered the sudden silence.
As everyone watched, frozen in their seats, he pulled
something out of a pouch at his waist: something
that shimmered with a ghostly
silvery hue, something that
jiggled and wriggled like a
living thing, and struggled
to escape from his cupped
palms.

With a slow, elaborate,
almost graceful gesture,
he moved his arms in a
wide arc, releasing a shining, silver

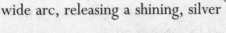

net that went spinning madly around the Tarasuns, encircling them completely.

The light of the Tarasuns dimmed instantly.

'MINE!' roared Shaap Azur. 'ALL MINE!'

'Let them go, Shaap Azur!' Shoon Ya's strong voice rang out from the front of the crowd. 'I COMMAND YOU!'

Shaap Azur giggled.

Somehow, the sound was even scarier than his roar.

'My *dear* twin brother,' said Shaap Azur mockingly. 'You *command* me? *Me?* You know as well as I do the power of the Silver Spinternet. Once it has been released, no power in the universe can control it.'

'That's not entirely true,' said Shoon Ya, striding confidently on to MegaStage and looking Shaap Azur fearlessly in the eye. 'Right, Shuk Tee?'

The petrified mithyakos breathed again. All was not lost as long as Shoon Ya was in control, surely.

'That is correct,' said Shuk Tee, who was close behind. She looked furious, and Shaap Azur would not meet her eye. 'The Spinternet has to be programmed before it is used. And the program should also specify the conditions for the release of the prisoners. Once those conditions are fulfilled, the Spinternet will automatically let its captives go.'

'Just as bright as ever, I see,' snarled Shaap Azur. 'Such a pity we're not on the same side. Together, we could've ruled Mithya, as equals, king and queen. But you! You chose to play second fiddle to my goody-two-shoes brother!'

He turned and spat on the stage. Then, turning to Shoon Ya, he continued, 'But I've always been the better programmer, Shoon Ya—you have said so yourself. And Taratrap 8.0 is one of my best ever, even if I say so myself. Plus, the conditions I have set for the release of the Tarasuns can *never* be fulfilled—not within the time frame I have set, anyway!' And he giggled again.

'Try me!' boomed Shoon Ya, exchanging a glance with Shuk Tee. She flipped a switch, and a huge screen popped up behind MegaStage. The words 'Transcriber Ready' began to flash on the screen. 'What are your conditions?'

Shaap Azur's eyes glazed over and he stared straight ahead. In a flat, robot-like voice, he recited his conditions. As he recited, the words came up on the screen behind, so that everyone could read them.

* On each of the eight worlds of Mithya, four riddles are hidden.
* Solving the four riddles will release the four Tarasuns of that world.
* All the riddles of one world must be solved before riddles of any other world become available.
* You can start with any of the worlds.
* Each set of four riddles has to be solved within eight octites.

or one octoll. The dingdial starts ticking the moment you click on that world on the Kay Laas Mithyamap.

* Exactly 24 dings after clicking on a world, the communication systems of that world will shut down. No summoner contact will be possible from that world to any other, or within that world itself.

* When the communication systems shut down, so will the gates. No one will be able to enter or leave that world until eight octites run out or the riddles are solved.

* Taratrap 8.0 times out at the end of one octet, or 16 octolls, starting now. If all the 32 Tarasuns haven't been released by then, Shoon Ya will admit defeat and take my place in the fiery lands beneath Dariya, and I, Shaap Azur, will become Emperaza.

* If these conditions are not accepted, Taratrap 8.0 will time out immediately and all the Tarasuns will die forever.

A shudder ran through the mithyakos. Even Shoon Ya's face turned pale under its rich nut-brown colour. If he didn't accept the conditions and the Tarasuns died forever, what would happen to Mithya and its people?

And if he did accept the conditions and failed to rescue all the Tarasuns within 128 octites, Shaap Azur would become Emperaza and the shadowy creatures of the Downsides would take over Mithya!

Both situations were too terrible to think about. The only way was to solve all 32 riddles within the time limit.

'I accept the conditions!' declared Shoon Ya. 'The

mithyakos of all eight worlds will work as one to rescue our beloved Tarasuns!' Turning to the crowd, Shoon Ya raised his staff.

'Are you with me, People of Mithya?'

The mithyakos got to their feet with a roar. 'YES, WE ARE!'

'Can we do this together, People of Mithya?'

'YES, WE CAN!'

'Will Tara shine again, People of Mithya?'

'YES, SHE WILL!'

'Humph,' said Shaap Azur in disgust. 'Always the popular one.'

Then a slow evil smile spread across his face. 'Cheer away, mithyakos! We shall see who's cheering at the end of the octoll.'

Hoisting the Spinternet onto his shoulder, Shaap Azur began to spin, until all that could be seen of him and the Tarasuns was a hazy multicoloured blur. As suddenly as he had appeared, he whirled through the floor of the stage and disappeared from view, taking the light with him.

For the first time in the eight trizillion octons of

Mithya's history, Kay Laas, Land of Eternal Taralite, Land of NeverNite, was plunged into darkness!

Little mithyakins began to wail. The crowd began to scatter in panic.

Suddenly, the huge screen on MegaStage, which had also gone dark, lit up again. The words 'PLEASE REMAIN CALM. PLEASE STAY SEATED' flashed on the screen.

The mithyakos obeyed. The emergency arcalamps, which had never been used on Kay Laas before, flooded MegaStage with light and warmth. As long as the arcalamps held out, Mithya would stay warm and bright, but theirs was a flat white light, an uncomfortably hot light, not the cool shimmering rainbow-coloured light of the Tarasuns. Everyone's hearts sank.

Then Shoon Ya spoke:

'People of Mithya, the Elders had predicted the Great Crisis. We had not expected it so soon, but we began preparations eight octons ago, when I became Emperaza, and we're ready. A Star Force has been put together, a group of people with special powers they do not know themselves. They will be the saviours of our universe. People of Mithya, please welcome—THE TARANAUTS!'

Crescent horns and conches sounded in unison. A thunderous applause broke out. Everyone cheered . . . and then looked around, confused.

Who were the Taranauts? And *where* were they?

Four

Tufan looked around him, wondering. This was brilliant—he had come to Kay Laas on a school trip and landed bang in the middle of the Great Crisis—super fun!

Then he saw it—in the front of the dark hall, close to MegaStage, there was a glowing golden halo! It was spotlighting a person—he couldn't see the person clearly, he was too far away, but from its height, it looked like a mithyakin, or a very short mithyakos. That was definitely one of the Taranauts!

He looked around, excitedly, and saw another similar halo, in the VIM seats of the Sparkl Area. That was the second one!

Excitedly, he grabbed a classmate and pointed. 'There,' he said, 'do you see them? Those halos of light? I bet those are the Taranauts, don't you?'

But his classmate just looked at him, open-mouthed. Out of the corner of his eye, Tufan saw Ms Kha Doos's jaw drop. He looked around, and noticed that everyone from Lustr Secondary, and everyone in the Lustr Area, really, was staring fixedly at him.

'What?' he said, suddenly nervous. What had he done *this* time?

He felt Ms Kha Doos's bony fingers in the small of his back, propelling him towards MegaStage.

He turned swiftly towards her, and it was then that he saw it—over his shoulder, all the way down his back . . . a golden light. He looked down at his fingers, at his feet in his favourite tattered sandals, and there they were, lit by the same glow.

Ms Kha Doos smiled at him. She looked almost pretty. 'Go on, Taranaut! Don't let Lustr Secondary down!'

Well, well, well. It had been a weird day all around,

but Ms Kha Doos smiling at him certainly took the cake. Hesitantly at first, then breaking into an excited trot, Tufan headed towards MegaStage.

Zarpa could not believe her eyes when she reached MegaStage. The other two Taranauts were Animal Boy and Scaredy Cat—the two mithyakins she had met in the Magmalift just half a ding ago!

They looked equally startled to see her—and each other.

Then Zvala, smiling a small relieved smile, quickly shuffled away from Tufan to Zarpa's right. Tufan took his place on her left. Already looking like a team, the Taranauts mounted MegaStage.

'Welcome, Taranauts!' boomed Shoon Ya.

The sound of anxious whispers came from the crowd. Why, the Taranauts were only mithyakins—they didn't  look more than nine or ten octons old, any of them! And they—these three nervous-looking mithyakins—would solve the riddles of Shaap Azur and save the Tarasuns? Fah!

Shoon Ya rested his strong arms lightly across the Taranauts' shoulders and looked at the crowd as if he could read their thoughts.

'People of Mithya,' he

boomed, 'the Taranauts go into mission training with me this dingling onwards. I invite you all back to Kay Laas exactly eight octites from now, to meet them again, and to be present at the launch of Operation T.A.R.A.—Taratrap Abort or Resolve Action.'

Coo-ool! Tufan had to make a real effort to look solemn and not break into a jubilant dance. He couldn't tell what Zarpa was thinking, but that silly Zvala was looking terrified. He could tell she would be absolutely no use as a Taranaut.

Shoon Ya hadn't finished. Letting the Taranauts go, he stepped to the front of the stage.

'Return to your homes now,' he announced, 'so that you can be safely in your beds before your worlds flip into Dariya for Taranite. Your Marazas and Maranis will have a Crisis Management Plan ready tomorrow morning at 3 o'ding sharp. Keep the faith, mithyakos! And stay alert!'

People began filing out quietly. Tufan tried to catch Shoon Ya's eye.

'Sir,' he said, reaching out to pet seaslith that had left Shoon Ya's arm and coiled itself affectionately around his neck. 'Sir, when can we start . . .'

But Shoon Ya was no longer listening— the Marazas and Maranis were waiting worriedly for him, and he had to go. Noiselessly, Shuk Tee stepped into the breach.

'All ready for mission training?' she asked.

'Yes, ma'am!' said Tufan instantly, clacking his heels to attention and saluting stiffly.

Shuk Tee smiled at his enthusiasm. 'Well, you need to get some sleep first. But at 3 o'ding sharp, your training begins!'

Zarpa sneaked a look at her dingdial. Half-past 29. Two and a half dings to Taranite. She was glad—she got very cranky when she didn't get her full quota of shut-eye!

'Will my Ma come along to be with me during training?' asked Zvala, in a small voice.

'No, Zvala, I'm sorry,' said Shuk Tee. 'Apart from your trainers, coaches, fellow Taranauts, and me, there will be no one else.'

Zvala gulped but held back the tears 'Can I say bye to her at least?'

'I would like permission to meet my parentsss too, Ms Shuk Tee,' Zarpa's voice lacked its usual chirpy tone, but it was clear and steady.

'Okay, but no more than five dinglings,' said Shuk Tee firmly. 'Everyone has to get back home before Taranite.'

Zvala raced away to Ma. 'Hey, Taranaut!' said Ma, giving her a big hug and holding her close, even though she was already getting very hot. 'I am so proud of you!'

Zvala sniffled into Ma's chest. 'But Ma,' she said. 'The other two seem so bold. And I just get scared about everything. What use am I going to be as a Taranaut?'

'*Hell-o?*' said Ma. 'Who has been the school topper for the last four octons? Who has such a sharp mind she wins all the Shyn scholarships? Bet you can crack Shaap Azur's riddles in a snap!'

Hey, Ma was right! T.A.R.A was not just about being brave, it was also about being smart. Zvala felt much happier. She wanted to crack those riddles *now*! 'Bye, Ma!' she said, squeezing out of Ma's hug and turning to go.

Then she turned around again. 'When you send me my clothes tomorrow, can you make sure you put in my silver sandals with the butterfly on top? And my orange jeans? And my aamberry-flavoured lip balm? And *do not* forget my little hand mirror and my hairbrush . . .'

Zarpa gave Mama and Papa a quick hug. She could see Papa was very distracted. His summoner was beeping incessantly.

'Remember to brush your hair sometimes, darling,' Mama was saying. 'And don't wear the same track pants for more than two days. And please, please be careful—I know you're very athletic and everything but sliding down hillsides and diving into racy rivers is not very sensible, you know . . .'

'All right, Mama,' Zarpa smiled. 'I'll be careful.'

'Let her be, Mama,' chided Papa. 'Our girl has been picked for a very, very important mission——now don't go putting all kinds of silly fears into her head!'

He placed his arms on Zarpa's shoulders and looked her in the eye. 'Go do it, Taranaut,' he said quietly. 'All the best!' Then he pulled out his beeping summoner. 'I have to run,' he sighed. 'It's the Marani.'

When Zvala and Zarpa returned to MegaStage, Tufan was standing right where they had left him. 'Don't you have to say bye to your parents?' asked Zvala.

'Um . . . my grandparents live in a small village in Lustr, and Dada is at the University of Glo,' said Tufan. He looked at the floor. 'My parents died . . .'

'Oops! I'm . . . I'm so sorry,' stuttered Zvala, embarrassed. 'I had no idea . . .'

Tufan did not look up. His covered his face with his hands. Oh, no! thought Zvala, beginning to get hot. Why was she always so stupid?

When Tufan spoke again, his voice trembled. 'You know what?' he said slowly. There was a long pause. 'Your feet are very red.'

He looked at Zvala's stunned face and burst out laughing. 'Got you!'

'You horrible boy!' cried Zvala, lunging at Tufan. He turned and ran, with a very red Zvala giving chase. Zarpa shook her head—it was going to be an interesting octoll. She hoped, for everyone's sake, that the three of them would be able to work well together.

'Ready to go, Taranauts?' Shuk Tee was striding across MegaStage. The makara trotted sedately in behind her.

'Yesssss, ma'am,' said Zarpa, stepping forward. Zvala and Tufan stood panting beside her, nodding.

'To the Palace, then!' commanded Shuk Tee. 'We shall meet again at 3 o'ding, to know more about your *true strengths* and *hidden powers*!' Mounting her makara, Shuk Tee headed off towards the Palace.

Escorted by an entire brigade of armed palace guards, the Taranauts marched in line behind her, a thrill of excitement running down their spines. What in the world did Ms Shuk Tee mean by their *true strengths*? What *hidden powers* did each of them have?

Five

At 8 o'ding precisely, Zvala and Zarpa marched into the circular tower room, the highest point on Mithya.

Zvala had been quite certain she would not be able to sleep without Ma tucking her in for the night, but the bed in the guest wing of the palace had been so soft and bouncy that she had slept for 16 straight dings without stirring. And then, it had been nice to wake up and see Zarpa sitting up in the other bed, grinning and ready for adventure. T.A.R.A. just might be more fun than she had imagined.

Through the windows that ran all around the room, the two Taranauts could see the endless expanse of Dariya, glimmering faintly in the glow of the arcalamps. Far and away in the distance were the bobbing silhouettes

of the eight worlds, all a uniform ghostly-white.

Two dinglings later, Tufan ran in, panting. 'Am I late?' he said breathlessly. 'I was in the shower . . .'

'Eeewwww!' said Zvala, crinkling her nose. 'What is that *stink*?'

'*Stink*?! You call that a stink?' said Tufan. 'I will have you know,' he continued, turning up his nose, and making a spritzing action with his thumb, "that it is 'what every well-groomed male is wearing".'

'Max Deo?' screeched Zvala and Zarpa together. 'That's meant for *older* people, not *you*!'

'Shhhhh!' said Zarpa, as footsteps sounded outside the door. 'Ms Shuk Tee is here!'

Shuk Tee walked in, dressed in deep crimson, her face lined with worry. She looked as if she hadn't slept at all. The Taranauts grew serious. This was not a fun adventure out of a storipad. This was the Great Crisis. And they had a huge responsibility on their shoulders.

'Take your seats!' commanded Shuk Tee. Then, stretching herself out to her full height—she was almost as tall as Shoon Ya himself—she began: 'You, Taranauts, are no ordinary mithyakins. Each of you possesses a unique ability that can help save the Tarasuns and Mithya.

'I had hoped we would have some time to train you well before the Great Crisis, but we have to do the best we can now. It is up to you to learn to use your abilities well and wisely in the very short time we have, or Mithya will be destroyed!'

There was a pause. Then Shuk Tee whirled on the three wide-eyed Taranauts. 'What do you think those talents are, Taranauts?'

'Well, I've always topped my class. Ma says I have a good mind . . .' offered Zvala.

'And she's always getting rather *hot and red* under the collar,' added Tufan. Zvala shot him a furious look.

'And I'm the bessst in my classss at Mulkum,' said Zarpa.

'And she has a very pronounced lissssp,' muttered Tufan under his breath, so that only Zvala could hear.

Zvala pointedly turned her back on him and didn't respond—she had noticed the strong lisp too but she wasn't going to be disloyal to Zarpa. Girls had to stick together!

'I can talk to most animals,' said Tufan, 'and identify at least 152 songs by the Lustr Blasters within the first ten seconds, and . . .'

'And he turns into a *high-pressure sprinkler system* at the oddest moments,' hissed Zvala, loud enough for Tufan to hear. He glared at her.

'All right, all right,' Shuk Tee snapped. 'I meant something else entirely. Maybe I'd better explain.'

'Zvala!' called Shuk Tee. Her voice resonated with energy, her body seemed to radiate light. Zvala stood up, awestruck. 'You are the child of Fire. When you learn to control your powers, you will have Fire's awesome ability to light up the night and warm people in the cold, as well as its amazing power to destroy!'

'Zarpa!' Zarpa shot to her feet. 'You are the child of Shay Sha, the SuperSerpent. When you learn to control your powers, you will have her legendary ability to protect her friends and destroy her enemies.'

'Tufan!' Tufan stood stiffly to attention. 'You are the child of the Wind. When you learn to control your powers, you will have both the breeze's gentle ability to revive and the hurricane's might to destroy!'

The Taranauts looked at each other with a new respect. Who would have thought it?

But Shuk Tee hadn't finished. 'At 4 o'ding, you will assemble at Zum Skar, the training centre where the bravest and brightest mithyakos have trained, to meet your coaches and trainers. I will meet you each evening at 28 o'ding, to review your progress. Remember we have only eight octites before we meet the people again and launch T.A.R.A., so do your best!'

Turning on her heel, she strode from the room.

The Taranauts broke into excited chatter. Of course it was Tufan who spoke first. 'The Mystery of the Red Hot Zvala—solved!' he grinned. For once, Zvala did not snap at him. She just nodded, her face full of wonder.

'That explains my weird running ssstyle,' said Zarpa. 'I go zig and zag and sssort of ssslide . . . actually, I ssslither . . . yes, that *exactly* what I do! And my pronounced lisssp—' she looked pointedly at Tufan, who turned red with embarrassment, '—is part of my hissss— so beware!'

'And you know, I kept getting sent home from school because weird things used to happen to my classmates when I got mad. I would start breathing hard and they would all go flying—they and the furniture too. No one could ever really prove anything, but they knew I was somehow responsible . . . Hey, Zvala— I can blow your fire out anytime!'

'You obviously don't pay attention in Mithscience class,' said Zvala snootily. 'A wind actually whips up a fire—fire gets its strength from the wind!'

Zarpa was lost in thought. 'But water can put out fire,' she said. 'Remember how when Tufan sort of "rained" on you, you cooled off immediately? I wonder where the water

comes into the wind thing . . .' Tufan looked at her, equally clueless.

'Eeeeeeee!' burst out Zvala. 'That's it! Don't you remember that song . . . Evaporation, condensation, water cycle, water cycle, followed by precipitation, water cycle, water cycle . . .'

The others looked blank.

'Did you feel sort of heavy when you reached the Magmalift after the hoverbus trip across Dariya?' Zvala asked Tufan.

'Yes, I did!' said Tufan. 'But how did you . . .'

'So-oh, since you have the power of wind, you were actually picking up the water that was evaporating from Dariya and carrying it with you. And when you reached a higher place, the top of Kay Laas, where it was much cooler, all the water droplets came together in you and condensed, and then, when you started laughing—you *rained*! No, seriously, you did!'

Tufan and Zarpa looked at Zvala admiringly. 'That's . . .' began Tufan, and hesitated. Then he continued, softly, 'That's pretty cool.'

Zarpa grinned to herself. The Taranauts might just work as a team, after all.

Then she glanced at her dingdial. 'Ten dinglings to 4 o'ding! We'd better start heading for Zum Skar, or we'll be late. Come on!'

Six

It was the eighth octite after Mithya had gone dark. Eight octites of not waking up to the many colours of glorious Taralite, eight octites of worrying, of wondering how three mithyakins could save Mithya from Shaap Azur and his Downsiders.

Thousands and thousands of mithyakos were gathered around MegaStage again, but this time, the mood was subdued. Worried mithyakos talked in whispers, shushing their babies.

The arcalamps were on in full force, radiating heat, and making the mithyakos sweaty and irritable.

Backstage, the Taranauts practised their moves nervously. They hadn't learnt to control their powers completely yet, but hopefully, what they had learnt would be enough to reassure the mithyakos somewhat, give them some hope.

More importantly, they each wanted to impress Shuk Tee. She was a tough taskmaster but she was fair and generous with her praise when it was deserved.

Zvala brushed her hair for the trizillionth time and peeked in her hand mirror. If she was going to be on MegaStage, she'd better look her best. This programme would surely be starcast live to all the worlds, and surely even Dana Suntana would be watching! Eeeeeeee!

Tufan fidgeted in the fancy long pants and full-sleeved shirt the girls had forced him to wear. He had only agreed to change out of his favourite long shorts with the Colourink spots and the faded Lustr Blasters tee when Zarpa promised he could borrow her way-cool, thumbnail-size Hummonica if he did.

Now, he smoothed the wafer-thin Hummonica onto his forehead, and quickly hummed the first bars of his ten favourite blast metal songs to create his playlist. The music began to play, booming directly into his head, so that no one else could hear. Feet apart, strumming an imaginary guitarele, Tufan began to headbang.

Zarpa had gladly swapped her Hummonica with Tufan for Squik and Chik-Chik. When she was tense and anxious, she preferred live things to gizmos, however cool. As she absent-mindedly stroked them and fed them zamunberries, she thought of Mama and Papa, and how she wanted to make them proud. As always, thinking of Papa helped her focus.

'Butterflies, Taranauts?'

The Taranauts snapped to attention.

They had all been so preoccupied with their own thoughts that they hadn't noticed Shoon Ya riding in regally from the wings. Bowing before the Emperaza, the Taranauts nodded.

'Well, take a few deep breaths and get set, because—' he threw out his arms in a grand gesture—'it's SHOWTIME!'

Crescent horns and conches once again sounded a merry fanfare as the curtains parted and Shoon Ya rode onto MegaStage on his shardula, followed by Shuk Tee on her makara. Shoon Ya dismounted, took centre stage, and raised his staff.

'People of Mithya!' he said, his voice ringing through the crowd. 'Welcome to Kay Laas! The last eight octites haven't been easy for any of us, but hope awaits.'

'Tonight, the Taranauts will display some—not all, mind you—of their astonishing and unique talents. When they have finished, we will together launch T.A.R.A by clicking on a world on the Mithyamap.'

'Please welcome, once again—THE TARANAUTS!'

The Taranauts marched in, heads held high—Zvala from left of stage, Zarpa from right of stage, and Tufan, freshly spritzed with Max, from the back. They assembled in the centre of the stage and bowed together.

Then Tufan and Zarpa took two steps back, leaving Zvala centrestage.

'PRESENTING, FROM THE WORLD OF SHYN—ZVALA!' boomed Shuk Tee.

The crowd applauded mildly. They were clearly not impressed by Shoon Ya's speech.

Zvala closed her eyes to shut them out. Getting worked up would ruin everything. The trick was to get the heat going without feeling tense. She emptied her head of all fear, all thought. She imagined a small flame burning right in between her eyes and focused only on it, just as her coach had taught her.

In a few dinglings, she could feel herself beginning to get hot. She felt herself grow hotter and hotter—and she was sure, redder and redder—until she knew she was ready.

Then she opened her mouth,

took in a large lungful of air, and exhaled. Dancing flames leaped out of her mouth and nostrils. The crowd gasped.

Zvala was thrilled. This was what Dana must feel like!

She whirled and twirled, and then stepped into an upright circular hoop. She stretched her arms. Out of her fingers leapt orange tongues of fire, setting the hoop alight, so that she was now in a perfect ring of fire. The crowd cheered.

She stepped out of the ring and picked up a block of wood. In two dinglings, all that was left of it was a little mound of ash. The crowd was on its feet now, clapping and cheering. Zvala bowed and stepped back.

'AND NOW, FROM SPARKL—ZARPA!'

Zarpa stepped forward. Her strategy of sending Zvala first had worked like a dream. People were always in awe of fire. The crowd was now suitably impressed.

A lilting, hypnotic tune began to play over the speakers. Zarpa closed her eyes and began to sway. She threw her arms back and bent backwards until her elbows touched the ground, then brought her head forward between her legs. Locking her hands around a pair of pillars that had been placed at one end of the stage, she began to stretch.

As the crowd watched, open-mouthed, she grew longer and longer and thinner and thinner, until her legs finally locked around another pair of pillars at the other end. The crowd gasped and cheered.

Then she let go, snapped back to her normal size like an elastic band, jumped to her feet, and zigged and zagged across the stage at such speed that all anyone could see of here was a blur. The crowd roared with approval.

Zarpa began to twist herself into all manner of pretzel shapes. She slithered up one of the pillars, and put all her years of Mulkum training on dazzling display—locking her feet around the pole and hanging horizontally off it, gripping the tiny tip of the pillar between her feet and winding her body around it. The crowd went wild.

Zarpa slithered down the pole, bowed, and withdrew.

'LAST, BUT NOT LEAST, FROM LUSTR— TUFAN!'

Tufan took centre stage, his head held high. Inside, though, his stomach was churning. All his life, he had been a complete nobody, a different kind of boy with few friends, who was constantly getting himself into trouble. This was his One Big Chance. He wasn't going to let anything ruin it.

Placing his feet apart, arms akimbo, eyes closed, Tufan began to breathe. The breathing, slow and quiet at first, began to get more rapid and much louder as he went along.

His chest began to heave like the seabed under Dariya, and awed mithyakos held their children tight as they began to be buffeted by huge gusts of wind. 'Hold on to your seats!' boomed Shoon Ya. Tufan's breathing grew faster and faster.

The doors of the hall burst open and the trees began to sway alarmingly. The wind howled and gusted. Leaves and dust swirled into the air, blinding the mithyakos.

Then, as suddenly as it had started, the wind died down. Tufan was now breathing softly again, his head going round and round. As he breathed harder, a tall, rotating column of air began to swirl in front of him, on

MegaStage. It was funnel-shaped and stretched from the ground to the sky.

The tornado began to swirl and move. Spinning faster and faster, it headed towards the pair of pillars at the edge of the stage, engulfed them, and lifted them clean off the ground! The crowd roared and stamped its feet.

Tufan breathed more slowly. The pillars spun slower and slower and finally came to rest in their original positions. Turning to the crowd, Tufan began to whistle. It was a low, haunting melody. A cool breeze began to waft gently over the crowd, soothing skins made itchy by the heat of the arcalamps. Babies stopped wailing and fell asleep. Mithyakos relaxed, and the worry lines disappeared from their faces.

Tufan bowed and retreated.

The crowd erupted into a deafening cheer. Shuk Tee flipped a switch. The gigantic screen went up behind MegaStage.

ShoonYa strode centre stage and raised his staff. 'Thank you!' he said. 'We have on our side the qualities of the fire and the wind, the ability to reach the deepest hidden secrets of Shaap Azur, and the sharp gifted minds of the three Taranauts . . . And now, to launch T.A.R.A., the Mithyamap!'

The map of Mithya came up on the gigantic screen. ShukTee clicked on the new 'Riddles' icon that had come up on the corner of the map. Instantly, each world was tagged according to the degree of difficulty of the riddles hidden in them.

'Which world would you like to start with, Taranauts?' asked Shoon Ya.

'Dif-fi-cult! Dif-fi-cult!' chanted the crowd. If the Taranauts cracked the toughest riddles when they were fresh and raring to go, the easy ones could be tackled even when they were tired!

Their confidence boosted by the crowd reaction, Zvala and Tufan turned to Zarpa. 'Yes,' they said eagerly, their faces alight with excitement. 'Let's crack Difficult first!'

'We will start with Easy, Emperaza,' said Zarpa calmly. 'And we will start with one of our home worlds, which at least one of us is familiar with. Please click on Shyn.'

'T.A.R.A. is now—officially—launched!' announced Shoon Ya. Shuk Tee clicked on Shyn. A map of Shyn appeared, with four blinking red dots indicating the location of the riddles.

A moment later, Shaap Azur's chilling giggle floated out of the speakers. 'Bay-bies, bay-bies!' he sang. 'Mithya can't be saved by babies!'

The crowd booed. Grateful for their support, the Taranauts smiled and waved. But they could not help feeling just a little nervous—what if Shaap Azur was right, and they could not save Mithya?

Seven

Excited and anxious at the same time, the Taranauts waited for the Magmalift to arrive. Nearly 18 dings were already gone since they had chosen Shyn—18 dings of getting final tips from their coaches, sitting in a final meeting with Shuk Tee, resting a little. They had to get to Shyn in the next six dings, before it closed down to the outside worlds.

Zarpa checked their kits for the trizillionth time. 'Map of Shyn, scroll of useful information, portalamps, enough stationery—palmyra to write on and scratchscribes to write with, brainfood bars, and . . . oh yes, of course, four *heavy* lexpads each . . .'

'What's *with* your world, anyway?' said Tufan to Zvala, irritably. 'Why doesn't everyone speak Taratongue, like all sensible mithyakos? No, you guys have to have four different provinces, where they speak four different languages, and no one can understand anyone else. And because you guys are such dunderheads, we have to lug all these lexpads along to interpret each language . . .'

'Oh, stop already!' hissed Zvala, looking dangerous. 'We have had exactly the same conversation about a hundred times, and the last one was exactly five dinglings ago.'

Luckily, before Tufan could respond, Shuk Tee arrived to see them off.

'I wish you could come with us, Ms Shuk Tee,' said Zarpa. 'With you in our team, we could have cracked the Shyn riddles and been back here in two octites, not eight.'

'Don't be so sure,' said Shuk Tee. 'You are the ones with the special talents, not I. And Zvala is one of the very few people on Shyn that speaks not only the language of her own province but also Taratongue, and that's very useful. I wish we could have been in touch by summoner, though.' Her face darkened. 'That was Shaap Azur's masterstroke—to cut you off from me. He knows I cannot leave Kay Laas . . .'

Then she smiled one of her rare smiles. 'But I can send someone *with* you.' The Taranauts looked at her, wondering. 'Take him,' she said, pointing to her makara. 'He has some useful talents, as I have no doubt you will discover . . .'

Tufan's face lit up. He scratched the ground with his foot, his shoe making a distinctive sound. The makara looked up at the boy, trotted over, and began to nuzzle him affectionately.

Tufan looked ecstatic. 'Hey, Makky,' he said.'

'Here's the Magmalift now,' said Shuk Tee, as it exploded out of the blowhole and landed gently by their side. 'There is an aquauto waiting for you at the station below. Makky will just swim along with you. Go on, hurry!'

The Taranauts and Makky hurried into the Magmalift, which was now back in position to take them down.

'So,' said Zvala, turning to Zarpa, 'how does the Magmalift go down?'

'Oh, it just uses gravity,' said Zarpa. 'But it fits very snugly within the shaft, and that's why we are not crashing to the ground.'

'Hey, Zarpa,' said Tufan suddenly, 'I've been meaning to ask. What happened to your lisssp? It has completely disappeared!'

Zarpa turned red. 'Well, when my coach asked me what I would like to learn first,' she mumbled, 'I said I'd like to lose my lisp. I'm afraid that was rather selfish of me—learning to control my lisp will not help Mithya—in fact, Mama thinks it's cute, but I . . .'

Zvala put her arm around Zarpa's shoulders and gave her a quick squeeze. 'You know what,' she said, sending a fierce glare in Tufan's direction, daring him to say another word. 'I would have done *exactly* the same thing in your place.'

For ten dinglings, they went down, down, down. Then the doors opened, and the Taranauts ran straight into the waiting aquauto. Half a ding later, they had reached the gates of Shyn.

❖

A huge cheering crowd of Shynkos, led by the Marani of Shyn, were waiting to receive them. There were representatives from each of the four different language groups, all holding placards and cheering lustily.

Zvala's should have been delighted, but she wasn't. She was home, but how different home looked without the beautiful green light of the four Shyn Emeralds!

Everyone in the crowd seemed to be talking at once. To Zvala, although she understood only one language, these were familiar sounds, but to the others, it sounded like pure noise.

'Uffpah! How in the world can you live here?' yelled Tufan into her ear, above the noise. Zvala and Zarpa glared at him and kept their best smiles on, waving and bowing.

But all three couldn't help heaving a sigh of relief as the gates of the Marani's palace closed behind them, and the noise faded.

'There's no time to lose!' said the Marani. 'Call in the Shynographers!'

Four Shynographers came into the room, carrying

detailed maps of Shyn and heavy lexpads. Each was from a different province of Shyn—and they neither knew Taratongue nor the languages of the other provinces. The Marani was the only one who could understand all of them.

'Upper right province!' barked the Marani. 'Have you located your riddle?' It was the province that Zvala came from.

'Yeles, yolour Stalarneless,' said the Shynographer of the Upper Right Province. 'Ilit ilis ilin thele bolox ilin thele Bolottolomleless Welell.'

'Oh no,' said the Marani in Taratongue, looking very worried. 'Shaap Azur has put the riddle in the box in the Bottomless Well. We have never been able to bring up that box, but we know it is there—because we can see it, as clear as Taralite!'

'I remember learning about it in MithLore class!' broke in Zvala. 'The well is bewitched, and when people try to descend it, the shaft just starts getting narrower and narrower. No one has ever been able to get to the box and back before the shaft becomes too narrow for them to squeeze through!'

'Oh, what are we going to do?' groaned the Marani, and began to wring her hands. The four Shyngraphers, who did not understand a word she was saying, began to wring their hands, too.

'How far from here is the Bottomless Well, Marani?' Zarpa's calm voice cut in. 'How long will it take us to get there?'

The Marani turned to the Shynographer. 'Holow falar?' she said. 'Holow lolong?'

'Halalf alan oloctalite tolo thele julunglele,' said the Shynographer.

'Half an octite by aquauto until you reach the Jungle of Jeopardy,' said the Marani. 'After that, it's anybody's guess. The jungle is dense and overgrown, so it depends on how quickly you can hack through it. The Bottomless Well is in the middle of the jungle, and the way to it is through a maze-like puzzle of paths, but there's only one that's actually leads to it.'

'Then we need to start immediately,' said Zarpa. 'Can the Shynographer of the Upper Right Province come with us to guide us along?'

'I'm afraid he won't be much use,' said the Marani. 'He is more a books and maps kind of guy, not an adventurous type.'

'Don't worry about that, Zarpa,' broke in Zvala. 'I've never been all the way to the Jungle of Jeopardy, but I know my way around Upper Right pretty well. We should be okay.'

'Can we dump the lexpads here then?' begged Tufan. 'For now? Since you know the language?'

'I guess so, and . . .'

'Maybe I should take a quick shower before we go? We have a long journey and . . .'

'NO!' said Zvala and Zarpa together. 'You just had one this morning. And before you ask, no, you cannot use any more deo either! Now come *on*!'

The Taranauts jumped into the waiting aquauto and waved goodbye to the Marani. She stopped wringing her hands just long enough to give them a thumbs-up. 'Bring back our Emeralds!' she smiled, but her voice cracked a little. 'And be careful, will you?'

The aquauto sped away, with the makara galloping rapidly beside on its short legs.

Zarpa glanced at her dingdial. 'Whoops!' she said. 'Two dinglings past communications systems shutdown!' She checked her summoner. It had gone completely dark. She looked around at her team. 'That's that, then, Taranauts. We are on our own.'

Eight

'Fellow Taranauts,' said Zvala grandly, 'Here's . . . The. Jungle. Of. Jeopardy!' It was the middle of the second octite after Shuk Tee had clicked on Shyn and sealed the Taranauts' decision. And Zvala was in a very, very good mood. The Taranauts had stopped off at her house to grab some food and some sleep, and Ma had stirred up a feast.

They had stuffed themselves with cheese-stuffed protlees and spicy goluchkas, and guzzled about three glasses of aamberry flipfloats. But Ma had saved the best for the last—a scrumptious galumpie, oozing chocolate from every pore. Then, when Shyn flipped over into Dariya and the Dar-Proofs came up and made Shyn watertight, Zvala had slept in her *own* bed after almost ten octites, used her *own* shower and tried on about ten different outfits in front of her own *full-length* mirror before deciding what she wanted to wear.

Ohhhhh yes, life was good.

Tufan was feeling pretty fine, too. He had absolutely loved the food at Zvala's, and had had a long, shower, finishing up with a generous spray of Max Deo.

Only Zarpa was worried. Dings were ticking away—and they hadn't even reached the location of the first riddle yet. She decided to take charge.

'Guys, let's look at the map now, and decide which route we should take. There seem to be several different entrances here, but which one is the right one?'

'That's fairly straightforward,' said Tufan, pulling at Makky's ears affectionately. 'It has to be Path G.'

'Right, let's go.' Hoisting their backsacks onto their shoulders, their portalamps in hand to light the way, and short-handled clippers to hack through the undergrowth, the Taranauts set off into the jungle. Makky trotted sedately behind them.

Just ten dinglings later, they stopped, frustrated. 'The portalamps are just not helping. It is far too dark in here,' sighed Zarpa. 'And the path is as overgrown as the rest of the jungle.'

'These clippers weigh about a hundred tols each,' said Tufan.

'And my hair has snagged on some trizillion branches already,' groaned Zvala.

'Oh, shut up!' Zarpa turned furiously on Zvala. 'It isn't the time to worry about your hair.'

Zvala's pretty face arranged itself into a sulk, but she kept quiet. Zarpa was right, of course.

'Hey, where did Makky go?' said Tufan suddenly. 'Makky! Hey, Makky!'

'Oh, leave Makky alone,' snapped Zarpa, going back to the map. Zvala had turned her back to the Taranauts and seemed very still. Makky came back, his snout working like a pair of bellows.

'Hey! That's it!' said Tufan. 'Makaras have a fantastic sense of smell! Makky can sniff out our path for us—I'm sure it has been used recently by animals or people. Or,' he paused, his voice dropping as he looked fearfully around, 'by Shaap Azur's Downsiders.'

There was a silence. Then Zarpa spoke. 'Anyway,' she said briskly. 'That's one problem taken care of.'

'And here's the other problem taken care of,' said

Zvala, turning around. She was glowing bright red, brighter than all three portalamps put together. She raised her right arm, closed her eyes, and went very still. Tongues of flame shot out of her fingers, and the jungle was suddenly as bright as Taralite.

'We don't need the clippers!' she exulted. 'I can just burn down the irritating branches and thorns!'

'No!' said Zarpa. 'You would start a full-blown forest fire that way! But maybe we can do a combination of hacking and focused burning.'

'I could help with that,' said Tufan. 'Let me blow the flames only along the path.' Then he turned to the makara. 'Makky, go!'

The makara ambled off, his snout to the ground, crashing through the undergrowth, following the twisting,

turning path with ease. The Taranauts allowed him a lead of about ten dinglings before they set out. There was no mistaking the path now that Makky's bulk had been through it.

'We have to do it bit by bit,' said Zvala. 'One straight stretch at a time. Every time the path curves, we have to start again. Let's try it!' Stretching her arms straight out in front of her, Zvala let the flames fly.

Behind her, Tufan inhaled, and then, standing on tiptoe, exhaled mightily from over Zvala's head. The rush of air sent the flames whooshing forward down the straight stretch of path in front of them and way beyond, burning everything in its path to ashes.

'Con-*trol*, Tufan!' yelled Zvala above the noise, trying to contain her flying hair with her hands. 'Control your breathing! You'll burn down the whole jungle if you don't!'

'Sorry!' said Tufan, with a sheepish smile. 'Let's go up to the next stretch and try again.'

This time, Tufan began by exhaling softly. Then he built it up slowly until the flames reached only until the point where the path curved again.

'Yayyyy!' cheered Zarpa. 'It worked! Now, looking at the map, we only have to do this a trizillion more times before we are at the Bottomless Well.'

'Whatever!' cried Tufan and Zvala, racing down to the next curve.

'Well, here we are—The Bottomless Well!' The Taranauts peered in over the wall around the well. 'And there's the box!'

Glinting up at them from the depths of the well, clearly visible through the crystal-clear water, was a slim metal cylinder.

'The well shaft looks wide enough to fit in a Magmalift!' said Tufan. 'Yes, but just put your arm into it and see what happens,' said Zvala.

Tufan stuck his arm into the shaft. For a dingling, it didn't seem as if anything was happening, but as they watched, the Taranauts saw the walls of the shaft moving in, so slightly that you could miss it.

Tufan quickly withdrew his hand, and the walls retreated. 'Wow!' he said. 'We have a problem.'

'Well, so far it has only been full-grown mithyakos who have tried going in. Maybe mithyakins like us can get through. We need a rope of some kind, though . . .' said Zvala.

Zarpa had been walking around the well wall, thinking. 'Let me do this,' she said suddenly. 'I don't need a rope.'

Zarpa climbed on to the well wall. Then hooking her feet over the edge of the wall, she went headfirst into the shaft. The walls began to move in.

Closing her eyes and focusing hard, arms extended in front of her, Zarpa began to stretch. And stretch. The walls continued to close in, tighter and tighter.

Zvala peered down the well shaft. 'Be careful!' she called anxiously.

Deep down inside the well shaft, Zarpa was worried too. Her arms were almost at the box, but the walls were very close now. She could feel the strain around her middle, and her arms felt as if they would tear themselves away from her shoulders any minute. That box had seemed so much closer from the outside.

'Con-cen-trate!' she told herself. 'Concentrate!'

She wondered if the walls had a limit, a point beyond which they couldn't close in. Already they were so close around her that it was becoming difficult to breathe. She certainly could not make herself much thinner—her body seemed to be at breaking point already.

'One last stretch!' she told herself. 'Go!'

Praying to Shay Sha the SuperSerpent to give her strength, Zarpa lunged for the box.

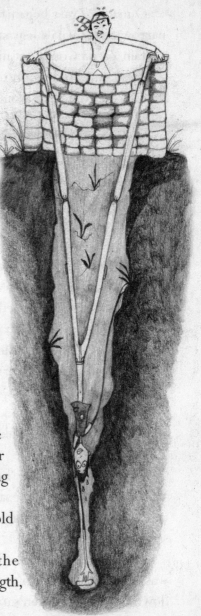

Outside, Zvala began to cry. The shaft was now so narrow and Zarpa's legs stretched so thin that she was certain Zarpa would not make it back up in time.

Tufan was holding on to Zarpa's feet. If she lost her hold on the edge, they would lose her forever. He glanced over at Zvala, irritated. How like a girl to blubber—As if that helped anything! He began to yell down the well shaft. 'Zarpa! Quit! Come out! NOW!'

The walls had almost completely closed in now. If Zarpa did not come up in the next dingling, the walls would squeeze the breath completely from her body!

TWAAAAAANG!

Tufan was knocked backwards to the ground with such force that it took him a couple of dinglings to figure out what had just happened. When he looked around, he saw Zarpa lying curled up on the grass a long way away, clutching a slim metal cylinder close to her chest.

'Are you all right?' cried Tufan, rushing over and shaking her.

Zarpa did not move.

'Zarpa! Hey, Zarpa! Wake up!' cried Tufan. Zvala stood by him, stony-faced.

Zarpa rolled over onto her back and began to mumble. 'She's saying something!' said Tufan, putting his ear close to Zarpa's mouth. 'I think she's saying . . . I think she's saying . . . *Got you*?'

'Got you!' cried Zvala, hooting with laughter. Zarpa was rolling on the ground, laughing till the tears ran down her cheeks. Tufan sat down, glaring at them. Then he began to laugh too. 'Good one!' he said. 'Now can we please look at the riddle?'

Riddle 1

The screw-top lid at one end of the cylinder opened easily. Inside was a rolled up sheet of palmyra. On it was a verse in Taratongue, written in shining emerald ink. Zvala smoothed it out and began to read.

Friendship is often
Called Amity too
Add an H—the universe
Will come to you
If you solve the riddle right
It will vanish out of sight

'Whaaaat?' said Tufan, grabbing the palmyra. 'Let me see.' He read it over again, slowly. 'I don't get it,' he said.

'I think it's pretty straightforward,' said Zvala. 'We add an H to the word amity and we get our answer.'

Zvala took out a palmyra and her scratchscribe from her backsack, and wrote it down. 'HAMITY? It doesn't mean anything,' groaned Tufan.

'Maybe if we scramble it up,' said Zvala, and started
to make a list:

* AHMTIY
* YITHAM
* HAYMIT
* IAMTHY

She looked at her palmyra from up close and from far
away. And then, suddenly, she had it.

'MITHYA!' she yelled with delight. 'MITHYA! Don't
you see it? *The universe will come to you*—Mithya is our
universe!'

'Hmmm. Maybe. But how can you be sure that you are
right?' said Zarpa. 'Let's look at the riddle again.'

She reached for the palmyra with the riddle but
something strange was happening to it. The words were
dissolving into a shining green star that glowed like a
miniature Emerald. As they watched, it rose out of the
palymra towards the sky and disappeared.

'It was right, then!' exclaimed Tufan. 'Remember
what it said in the last two lines—'If you solve the riddle
right, it will vanish out of sight!'

'Yay!' cheered the Taranauts, doing a victory jig around
a very surprised Makky. 'One Emerald down, I mean, *UP*,
and only three to go!'

Nine

The Taranauts were on their way to the Upper Left Province. They had spent another Taranite at Zvala's—sleeping and stuffing themselves silly once again—and now, they were all ready to take on the next challenge.

Their backsacks were heavier this time—weighed down as they were with their lexpads.

'I simply do not see,' grumbled Tufan, 'why each of us has to carry a lexpad when one is plenty.'

'Because,' explained Zvala through gritted teeth, 'if we have to split up to get information, we would feel like perfect idiots if we each did not have one.'

'So,' said Zarpa, when they were all settled in the aquauto, 'time to look at the map. We're off to the seaside town of Sandistan.'

'Yeah,' sighed Zvala, 'great beach, emerald waters . . . but no Tarashine . . .'

'No point moaning,' shrugged Tufan. 'that's why we're here, remember—to bring the Tarashine back. Hey, that would make a cool song: 'Briiiiing the Tarashine baaack, baaaybeee, bring it baaack to meeee' . . .'

'Enough already, you two!' snapped Zarpa. 'Back to the map!'

'Now here are the directions to the riddle,' she continued, unscrolling the palmyra they had got from the Shynographer of the Upper Left. 'And this is as far as I've got in translating it. 'The riddle is hidden in a bottle, and the bottle is buried on the beach . . .'

'Ok, but where? It is a very long beach!'

'Yes, yes,' said Zarpa exasperatedly. 'There are more directions here. But now we need a lexpad. It says 'Buput fipirst thepe mopuviping fipirewapall hapas topo bepe croposspoed.'

'Okay. Let's see now..,' said Zvala, struggling to turn the pages of her lexpad. They were very thin and it was

really hard to turn them one page at a time.

'*But first the moving firewall has to be crossed*,' read Zarpa, when all the words had been translated. 'But what *is* a moving firewall, anyway?'

'Oh I know!' exclaimed Zvala. 'it is an invisible wall along the coastline that keeps changing its location every Taranite, when the Taratide comes in! We'll have to reach Sandistan, look up the daily bulletin at the town hall, and figure out exactly where it is today. *Then* we will have to get beyond it, and *then* start looking for the bottle! If we don't crack this one by Taranite, we'll have to start all over again tomorrow!'

Zarpa looked at her dingdial. 'We should be getting to Sandistan in half a ding,' she said. 'And Tufan, let's leave Makky in the Sandistan stables this time—I don't think the people of the town are going to appreciate a ginormous makara galumphing through their streets.'

Sitting on a bench outside the Town Hall of Sandistan and sucking on giant sweet-sour imlichis, the Taranauts pored over the map of the town and the directions to the firewall's location that octite.

'*Take . . . the . . . northeast . . . road . . . from . . . the . . . Sand . . . Plaza . . . Turn . . . off . . . on . . . the . . . second . . . road . . . going . . . due . . . south,*' said Zvala, translating from her lexpad.

'More translations!' groaned Tufan. 'I'm sorry but I shall have to say it again. The people of Shyn need to get their heads examined!'

Zvala did not bother to answer. She just cuffed him over the head and continued: '*Beyond . . . the . . . park . . . take . . . the . . . dirt . . . track . . . that . . . heads . . . . southeast . . . to . . . reach . . . the . . . firewall.*'

The three heads pored over the map again. 'I know where the firewall is!' yelled Zarpa and Zvala together.

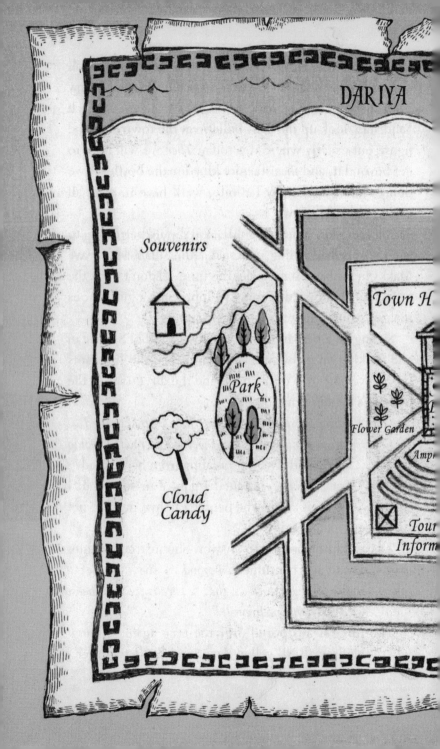

DARIYA

Souvenirs

Park

Cloud
Candy

Town H

Flower Garden

Amp

Tou
Inform

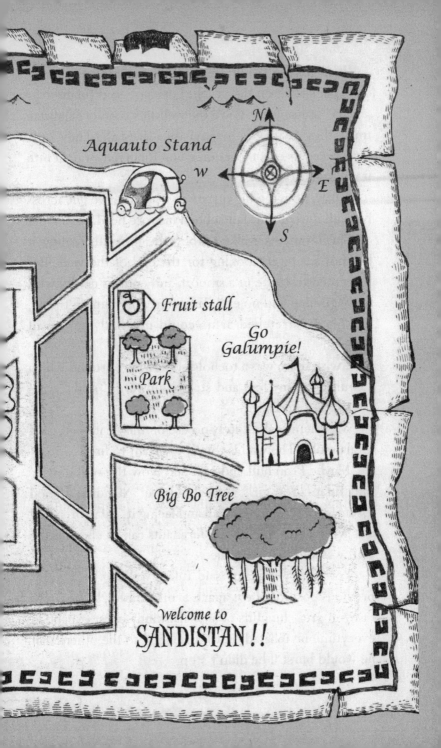

'It's between the Bo tree and the galumpie parlour!'

'That's right on the beach! Let's go!' said Tufan.

The Taranauts ran down the well-lit streets of Sandistan until they reached the invisible firewall. They only discovered its exact location when Tufan ran straight into it and bounced back.

'Okay, now the big question—how do we get across it?' said Zarpa, as Tufan rubbed his sore head.

The Taranauts walked along the firewall, feeling it but not seeing it, looking for the end of the wall. But it seemed to curve in a smooth and endless circle, with no beginning and no end. Tufan stretched up on tiptoe, but his outstretched arms could not find the top of the wall.

'I wish there was a toehold somewhere around which I could lock my feet and stretch upwards,' said Zarpa, 'But I can't find any.'

'My talent is absolutely no use on this challenge,' said Zvala sadly. 'The wall is totally resistant to fire.'

'Maybe I can huff and puff and blow the wall down!' said Tufan. 'You girls get behind me!' Standing a good distance away from the wall and facing it, Tufan breathed out with all his might. The Taranauts ran to check if the wall was still there. It was.

'Let me try it again,' said Tufan, walking back to his previous position. Legs apart, arms akimbo, he began to draw in great lungfuls of air. His skinny chest expanded everytime he inhaled, until it seemed to the others that he would burst if he didn't stop.

Then, becoming very still, he let it all out in a great *whooooosh*. The sand on the beach in front of them rose up in a giant dust storm several gigafeet high, crashed into the wall, and rebounded on the Taranauts.

When Tufan looked around, Zvala and Zarpa were nowhere to be seen!

Two dinglings later, they surfaced from under two identical sand dunes that the Tufan storm had just created, coughing and spluttering. 'Do you want to bury us alive, silly?' snapped Zvala.

'How was I to know that would happen?' snapped back Tufan, tired now and irritated that all his effort seemed to have had no impact on the wall. It was only one ding to Taranite now and they hadn't even got past the wall yet.

'Hey, come here and look!' It was Zarpa, and she was calling excitedly from near the firewall. 'We kept trying

to go *over* the firewall or *around* the firewall, but we never tried to go *under* it! And Tufan's blowing has blown the sand off this little passage going under the wall. Taranauts, I believe we have found our way to the other side!'

Getting down onto their stomachs, the Taranauts wiggled their way under the firewall and to the other side.

'Now to find the bottle!' said Zarpa. 'Tufan, you will have to start blowing again!'

Tufan started to breathe out hard again. The sand swirled around them and rearranged itself in different patterns, but the bottle was not to be found. 'I can't keep this up much longer,' said Tufan. 'I'm getting tired. And Taranite is almost here. You guys need to help.'

'Time for a little ziggy-zaggy!' cried Zarpa, and began speeding over the sand faster than the eye could see. Along the furrows she created, all kinds of things began to reveal themselves—shells, a long-buried shoe, coins, the tip of a child's sand-shovel . . . Zvala, her fingers shooting fire and light, kept an eagle eye on the ground, until she saw something glinting in the firelight—was it . . . yes, it was!

'The bottle!' she screeched. 'The bottle!'

'Let's get back to the other side of the wall first!' cried Zarpa. 'Or we shall get stuck here and when we get out tomorrow, who knows where we will be?'

'The passage's gone!' groaned Tufan. 'With all the blowing and zigzagging we've been doing, we've managed to cover it up again!'

'One last blow, Tufan,' begged Zarpa. 'Do it again or we will lose another octite!'

Drawing on every last ounce of strength left in his lungs, Tufan began to inhale. Sweat poured down his face and neck. When his chest seemed about to burst, he closed his eyes, crossed his fingers, hoped for the best, and *blew*!

'There it is!' yelled Zvala. 'You did it, Tufan!'

Quickly, the Taranauts wiggled into the passage and out on the other side, Zvala clutching the bottle. Stopping only a moment to breathe a sigh of relief, they turned their attention to the bottle. It was round, like a ball, and milky-white, so you couldn't see through it.

'Weird,' said Zarpa. 'It doesn't seem to have an opening of any sort.'

'Just smash it against something,' said Tufan wearily.

But no amount of smashing had any effect on the bottle. Less than half a ding left to Taranite, and they had strict orders to be in their beds at the Sandside Motel by the time Shyn flipped into Dariya.

Then Zvala had a brainwave. 'Heat! Heat will crack glass if nothing else will!'

Closing her eyes, she began to warm up. She got hotter

and hotter. Suddenly, with a loud crack, the bottle in her hand split into two!

'Riddle 2!' cried the Taranauts, lunging for the palmyra.

Riddle 2

Add the first two of a little horse
To the last two of what is
    not more
Add the dress, but not the doctor
Then run away, but leave the cape
    at the door
If you solve the riddle right
It will vanish out of sight

The Taranauts read the riddle over and over. Then Zvala took out her palmyra pad and scratchscribe. 'Okay, what's a little horse?'

'Foal!'

'Pony!'

'So the first two letters are either FO or PO. Let's go on. *What is not more?* What does that mean?'

There was a silence. 'This is probably silly,' said Tufan. 'But I can only think of LESS. Less is *not more*, right?'

'Perfect!' cried Zvala in delight, thumping him on the back. 'Last two letters of less. So we have FOSS or POSS . . .'

'Add the dress, but not the doctor'—that's soooo random. What does it *mean*?'

'Maybe it is a dress the doctor wears—like an apron, or a surgical mask, or something?'

'Or . . . HEYYYYY! Dr is short for Doctor, right, so if you take away DR from dress, you are adding the dress, but not the doctor! So we have FOSSESS or POSSESS. I think I'm going with POSSESS.'

'I think I cracked the last one,' said Zarpa excitedly. 'Run away—what's another word for 'run away'? ESCAPE! But leave the cape at the door. That means just ES without the CAPE. So we have POSSESSES!'

'Ok, so it's a real word, but what is the connection with the first riddle?' frowned Zvala. 'Is there a connection at all?'

'Never mind now!' said Zarpa, pulling her to her feet and looking at the riddle palmyra. A glittering green star was lifting off it and beginning to head skywards. 'What matters is that we've rescued Emerald number two!'

Then she looked at her dingdial and let out a horrified shriek. 'Ten dinglings to Taranite! On your marks, get set . . . zip!'

Ten

The Taranauts were sitting around the breakfast table, tucking into the crispest, butteriest creposas ever. 'Eeeeeeeeeeee!' shrieked Zvala so loudly that Zarpa jumped out of her skin and Tufan dropped his chocolate flipfloat all over his Lustr Blasters T-shirt.

'*What* happened?' he asked furiously.

'We are in the *Sandistan Times*! Front page! We're celebrities!'

'Already?' said Zarpa, frowning. 'What does it say?'

'Ahem,' Zvala cleared her throat slowly and deliberately. '*Taranauts Crack Sandistan Riddle: Last evening, just four octites after Operation T.A.R.A. was launched, the Taranauts solved the second of Shaap Azur's 32 riddles. With this breakthrough, there remain only two more riddles still*

hidden on Shyn that have to be solved in the next four octites. The Taranauts' performance so far has brought a glimmer of hope to mithyakos, who have been in despair since the Tarasuns were seized by Shaap Azur on the occasion of the Octoversary. If the Taranauts succeed in solving the next two riddles, we could have our Shyn Emeralds shining down on us very soon indeed.'
She looked around, preening, at the other two.

'Wow!' said Tufan, grinning widely. Zarpa frowned. 'How did the news get out so quickly? We just made it back to the motel before Taranite! Did either of you…?'

'Well, I just mentioned it to the guy at the reception,' shrugged Zvala.

'Maybe we should keep it quiet for now,' said Zarpa.

'Oh Zarps, you are *always* worried about something,' said Tufan.

'I kno-ow,' said Zarpa hesitantly, 'but…'

'What's done is done,' said Tufan matter-of-factly. 'Now let's figure out the Lower Left Province—that's where we're headed today, right?'

'Right,' said Zvala, taking charge. She was feeling guilty about blabbing to the motel receptionist and wanted to make amends. 'Zarpa and I will try to make some sense of the map and get started translating the directions the Shynographer of the Lower Left gave us. Tufan, why don't you run along and get Makky from the stables in the meanwhile? Let's aim to leave in half a ding.'

Half a ding later, the Taranauts were in an aquauto speeding towards the Lower Left, Makky galloping along behind them, sneezing mightily. The poor makara had caught a cold from animals in the neighbouring stables and looked miserable.

'Okay, so this time, it is going to be just a bit more challenging,' said Zarpa, 'because the Shynographer himself isn't quite sure where the riddle is hidden. All he knows is an approximate location—the Fertile Fumpgourd Fields. Where the fumpgourd fields are—'she pulled out her lexpad, 'we still have to find out. This is it . . .'

'Beseyosond these Casastesle osof Cosonfususision lisie these fusumpgosourd fisields. These eiseight keseys toso these gasate asare isinsiside these casastesle. Pisick thesum usup isin these risight osordeser osor these gasate wisill nosot osopesun.'

'That reads,' said Zvala finally, '*Beyond the Castle of Confusion lie the fumpgourd fields. The eight keys to the gate are inside the castle. Pick them up in the right order or the gate will not open.*'

'What *is* the right order, though?' said Tufan.

'I suppose we will find out when we get there,' yawned Zvala. She had woken up very early to wash the beach sand out of her hair and skin, and she was sleepy now. 'I'm going to take a nap.'

❖

'Wake up, Zvala!' Zvala jumped. Tufan was yelling in her ear and obviously enjoying the effect it was having. 'We're there!'

'All right!' she snapped irritably, getting out of the aquauto. They were standing outside a grove of extraordinarily tall trees. 'But where is the Castle?'

'Beyond the Forest of F-e-a-r,' hissed Tufan.

'Really?' said Zvala. Her face had turned pale.

'Shut up, Tufan,' Zarpa gave him a friendly shove. 'He's just fooling. But apparently it is very easy to lose your way in this grove, so the aquauto guy doesn't want to take us any closer.'

'How kind of him,' said Zvala, annoyed. 'Now how are we supposed to find our way to the Castle?'

'We are the Taranauts, we will find a way,' announced Tufan grandly, whipping out his compass, scratching the sneezing makara's ears, and leading the way.

Two dings later, they had walked several milyards but were back where they had started. The grove was well-lit but all the paths looked exactly the same. The compass had failed completely for reasons they could not explain. Makky's cold had completely destroyed his sense of smell—he looked forlorn and was happy just following Tufan around.

'Ideas, anyone?' Tufan looked defeated.

'Maybe if one of us climbed a tree and looked around...' suggested Zvala, her tone indicating that she definitely was not going to be the one.

'Good idea,' said Zarpa and Tufan together. 'I'll do it!'

In two dinglings, they had shinned up a tall, tall tree like little monkapis. 'I see the lights of the castle,' called

Tufan, 'and I can see the way leading to it as well. But I can only see it from up here…'

'Guide me and Zarpa there, then,' yelled up Zvala.

'Very funny,' retorted Tufan, 'and how am I supposed to find my way there afterwards?'

'That's the point,' grinned up Zvala. 'You don't!'

'Guys, guys, get serious,' said Zarpa. 'Maybe I can lock myself around one of these trees here and stretch along the path that Zvala is walking, and lock myself on the other side as well, and Tufan can use me as a guide. Then I can snap to the Castle.'

'No, Zarpa,' said Tufan. 'I don't think you are strong enough yet to stretch that far. We need to think of something else.'

'Tell you what,' said Zvala, 'I will leave a little scorch mark on each of the trees we pass. You just need to follow the marks.'

'Brilliant,' said Tufan. Zarpa quickly shinned down the tree.

Zvala closed her eyes, imagined a little flame in the centre of her forehead, and focused on it. As she did, she felt herself grow hotter and hotter. Soon she was ready.

Tufan yelled out instructions and the girls followed, Zvala resting her scorching hand on each tree that they passed.

Half a ding later, all three were at the front door of the Castle of Confusion, peering at the map of the inside. They had 'hallo'ed endlessly and looked all around, but no one seemed to be around.

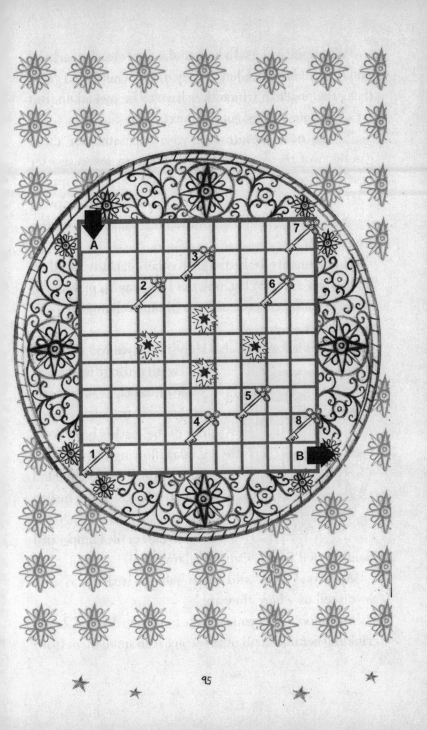

'Where each key is to be found is very clearly marked,' said Zarpa. 'And each key is tagged with a number. I guess that's the order in which they have to be picked up. But let's translate the instruction next to the map...'

'"Doso nosot resetrasace yosuur pasath osor these gasates osof these casastsele wisill shusut fosoreseveser besehisind yosuu".'

'Do...not...retrace...your...path,' translated Zvala slowly, 'or...the...gates... of... the... castle...will... shut . . . forever... behind...you.'

The Taranauts looked at each other fearfully and then at the map again. What was the best way to pick up all the keys in the correct order without walking the same path twice?

'I've got it!' said Zvala. 'Here's how we will do it.'

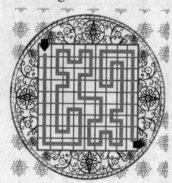

Twenty dinglings later, with all the eight keys safely in her pockets, Zarpa walked out of the castle's back door, Zvala following close behind. Tufan brought Makky around from the front, where he had left him.

'To the Fertile Fumpgourd Fields,' cried Tufan. 'Onward, Taranauts!'

'Aye, aye, Cap'n,' said Zarpa, saluting smartly, 'as soon as you tell us where they are.'

'Yuckthoo! Can't you *smell* the fumpgourds?' said Zvala, crinkling her nose. 'All of us on Shyn can smell them from a trizillion milyards away, they *stink*. Actually,' she paused, sniffing, 'they smell like something familiar...'

Zarpa caught on instantly. 'Max Deo!' she yelled.

Shrieking in mock fear, the girls ran towards the gates of the fumpgourd fields, Tufan in hot pursuit, and Makky, his spirits revived, galloping happily alongside.

All the keys turned easily in their slots. The gates swung open noiselessly, and the Taranauts stopped short. In front of them were vast fields, several ectacres wide, full of fumpgourds, small and big, in every colour from raw blue to ripe violet.

How were they ever going to find the riddle here?

But Makky seemed very, very excited. The strong rotten smell of the fumpgourds seemed to have cleared his airways beautifully, and he was away into the fields before they could stop him, rooting among the gourds, completely ignoring the blue ones and nibbling away at the ripe violet ones, sucking up their slimy insides.

As they watched, wondering what to do next, Makky stopped suddenly, his snout working overtime. He seemed to be very puzzled by a larger-than-usual blue fumpgourd. He would sniff at it, then go away for a bit, look at it from a distance, growl in his throat, and then come galloping back to attack.

Tufan looked at him, frowning. 'Taranauts,' he said slowly. 'I think we might have found our riddle.'

The Taranauts raced to the blue fumpgourd. It was much lighter than the others, and was made of a thin, fragile-looking material.

'Smash it?' asked Zvala.

'Smash away!' said Zarpa.

Holding it high above her head, Zvala smashed the fumpgourd to the ground. The 'gourd' smashed into smithereens.

In the middle of the debris was a scroll of palmyra.

Riddle 3

From half of Taralite's dings
plus a quarter of Taranite
Take half a score and ten
It's easy! It's nothing! That's right!

'Hmmm,' said Zarpa. 'So half of dings is . . . *din*? Or is it *ing*? Or is it *ngs*?'

'And a quarter of Taranite has so many possibilities,' groaned Tufan. 'Could be Ta, or Ra, or Ni, or Te . . .'

They all looked at the palmyra for a long moment.

'Unless,' said Zvala, her eyes gleaming, 'the riddle is talking about *numbers*, not letters!'

'You mean, like half the *number* of dings in a Taralite?' said Tufan.

'Exactly!' said Zvala. 'So we know that a Taralite has 32 dings in all, so half that number is . . .'

'16!' yelled Zarpa. 'And Taranite has 16 dings, so a quarter of that is 4.'

'It says '*plus* a quarter', so we add up 16 and 4 and get . . . 20,' Tufan chimed in.

'Brilliant,' cried Zvala. 'Yes, the words are very important here. See, in the next sentence, it says "take half a score"—I'm guessing that means "take away".'

'Ok, we'll go with that,' said Zarpa. 'So from 20, *take away half a score and ten*—anyone know what a score is?'

'20,' said Zvala instantly. 'A score is twenty. So half a score is 10.'

'So we add half a score—10—*to* ten—which gives us 20 again, and then we take it away from 20, and we are left with . . .'

'Zero!' they all chorused together.

'And that's what the riddle says—'It's nothing!' Nothing is the same as zero. Which means zero is the right answer!' yelled Tufan.

This time, none of them needed to look at the ascending green star to know that they had got the right answer. But Zvala was still looking at the answers to the three riddles they had now cracked—Mithya; Possesses;

Zero. If there was a connection between the three words, she still hadn't a clue what it was.

Meanwhile, Zarpa was already looking at her dingdial. 'Good work, team!' she said. 'Now let's get to the Lower Left Circuit House before Taranite.'

'Yes,' sighed Zvala, 'time to start looking for the scorch marks again . . .'

'Or,' said Tufan, smiling, 'since Makky's brilliant sense of smell is back, we could just take the Makkybus!'

The girls looked at him, puzzled.

'Kneel, Sir Makky!' commanded Tufan. Makky knelt.

'Come on aboard, girls!' said Tufan. The girls squealed with delight.

Two dinglings later, they were bouncing through the grove on the back of the makara, who headed unerringly for the waiting aquauto on the other side of the grove.

Eleven

'All right, everyone,' said Zarpa over breakfast. She looked exhausted. 'Two octites to go and the last riddle to be found and cracked!'

'Yay!' said Tufan, without much enthusiasm. Zvala pumped her fist in the air, rubbed her eyes, and yawned.

The Taranauts were not a cheerful lot this morning. Their beds at the Lower Left Circuit House had been lumpy and infested with tiny keedaboochis, which had kept them awake and scratching for most of the night. The rock-hard biddlies and the extra-spicy chukambar for breakfast hadn't helped.

'Snap out of it, guys!' urged Zarpa. 'Think about it! If we do this, by the end of day tomorrow, Tarashine will be back—at least an eighth of it. And we will be on our way home!'

'That's true!' Zvala cheered up immediately. 'By tomorrow, the Shyn Emeralds will be back if everything goes well! And I will go hooooooome!'

Only Tufan still looked sulky. Going home to Azza and Azzi was not really the most exciting thing in the world, and the Tarashine from the Emeralds would barely reach his southern world of Lustr, anyway. Zarpa and Zvala looked at each other, shrugged, and opened the map of the Lower Right Province. They had no more time to lose.

'Ok, we're headed now for the Crisscross Cavern at the far end of the Lower Right. The riddle is hidden in it,' said Zarpa.

'Really?' Zvala looked worried. 'I remember it from Shynography. It is very far away and is not easy to get to.'

'Let's start rightaway, then,' said Zarpa, picking up her backsack, and handing Zvala and Tufan theirs. 'To the aquauto, team!'

The Taranauts jumped into the aquauto and promptly fell asleep.

Three dings later, Zvala woke up, feeling very rested. She looked affectionately at her sleeping teammates and smiled. Then she looked out of the window, watching the unfamiliar scenery and marvelling at all that had happened to her since the Octoversary.

'Eeeeeee!'

Zarpa and Tufan jumped, suddenly awake.

'I wish you would *stop* doing that!' said Tufan crossly. 'What is it now?'

'The cutest little café!' said Zvala. 'Let's stop— I'm starving!'

Half a ding later, stuffed to the gills with the kind of junk their moms would never have allowed at one sitting—flaky puffboos, crisp batatafries, and two bottles of pepcofizz each—the Taranauts were in much better spirits. So was Makky, who had made a glorious meal of a pile of overripe fumpgourds that the café owner had put aside for the trashman to pick up. 'Uh-oh . . .'

'Let's crack the directions,' said Tufan, opening the map and reaching for his lexpad.

'All-*right*, all-*right* . . . uh-oh . . .'

'What happened?' said Zvala.

'I forgot to change my lexpad,' said Tufan. 'I still have the Lower Left one. I hope you changed yours?'

The girls looked at each other, horrified. They had been so sleepy and crabby this morning that they hadn't remembered to change *their* lexpads either. They looked down at the instructions:

'Sadail adocrodoss thede Ladaughiding Ladake, adand crodoss thede Rodockidy Pladainids, fodollodowiding thede sidigns.

'It's pure gobbledegook!' groaned Zarpa. 'What are we going to *do*?'

They looked at the instructions again for a long moment. Then Zvala had a brainwave. 'Let's pull out yesterday's instructions and the translation. Maybe there is some pattern to the languages, or common words . . .'

'Here it is. So, 'Doso nosot resetrasace yosuur pasath osor thesu gasates osof these casastesle wisill shusut fosoreseveser besehisind yosuu' translated to 'Do not retrace your path or the gates of the castle will shut forever behind you,' she said. 'Are there words in today's directions that are somewhat familiar?'

'Well,' said Tufan, 'Thede' is somewhat similar to 'these', I guess. And 'odof' is similar to 'osof'.

'Okay, we know that 'these' translates to 'the' and 'osof' to of. What if 'thede' also translates to 'the' and 'odof' to 'of'? Then the difference between the two languages is only the use of 'd' instead of 's'!'

'You've probably got it!' squealed Zarpa. 'If you look at yesterday's instructions and the translation carefully, there just seem to be more letters in the Shyn language words than in Taratongue. See—'Doso' translates to 'Do'—so we just remove the so, 'nosot' translates to 'not', again we just remove the 'so', 'resetrasace' translates to 'retrace', remove the se and the sa . . .'

'So in today's instructions, if our theory is right, we simply remove the 'd' and the vowels—a, e, i, o, u—after or before it from every word, and we should have the instructions in Taratongue!' cried Zvala. She pulled out a palmyra sheet and her scratchscribe. 'Let's try it!'

'We have it!' shrieked Zvala. 'Sail across the Laughing Lake, and cross the Rocky Plains, following the signs!'

'Eeeeeeee!' said Tufan, quickly ducking a punch from Zvala.

Then he raised his arms over his head and bowed dramatically. 'All hail to the dunderheads of Shyn, who spend their entire lives not understanding each other or the rest of Mithya, when they are all actually speaking the same language!'

'I suppose I cannot disagree with that,' Zvala smiled wryly. 'We are quite the dimwits, aren't we?'

'The Laughing Lake!' announced Zarpa, as the aquauto came to a halt.

The Taranauts jumped off the aquauto and gazed at the endless water shimmering in the light of their portalamps. In a dingling, Makky had dived in and begun splashing about happily, making small noises that sounded suspiciously like chuckles.

'Back into the aquauto!' called Zvala. 'Let's go!'

The aquauto zoomed across the lake, Makky swimming behind. The Taranauts looked at each other and began to giggle helplessly.

'I wondered why it was called the Laughing Lake,' gasped Zvala, dissolving into giggles again. 'Now I know!'

'Uh-oh,' said Tufan, raising his arms, which had begun to feel fat and heavy, and giggling. 'It's happening again!'

'Eeee-vaporation, condensation, water cycle, water

cycle . . . ,' sang Zarpa and Zvala together, hooting with laughter.

By the time the aquauto had reached the other side of the Laughing Lake, the Taranauts were really tired. Makky, who had been giggling all the way across, looked worn out too.

'Tufan,' said Zarpa, darting a glance at her dingdial. 'We can't take a break. We just *have* to cross the Rocky Plains now, and fast. There's no way the aquauto can get through these rocks. Do you think we could take the Makkybus?'

'We-ell,' said Tufan, fondling the makara's ears. 'He looks all in. But he can still take us across much faster than we can get there ourselves. I am so heavy right now I can barely walk. What say, Makkyboy?'

The makara looked adoringly at Tufan and nuzzled him. He would do anything for the boy.

'To the Makkybus!' said Tufan. In a trice, they were trotting along at a decent pace. The path was well-lit and well marked, and they had no trouble at all.

'It's good that Makky is too tired to go any faster!' said Zvala. 'The ride is bumpy enough at this pace, with all the rocks along the path!'

'Here we are!' announced Zvala. 'The sign says Crisscross Cavern, and it is pointing this way. That was simple!'

Zarpa had been glancing worriedly at her dingdial. 'Yes, but getting here took much much longer than it should have. We have to be out of here in half a ding if we want to get to the bed-and-breakfast place we are supposed to stay at before Taranite!'

The Taranauts jumped off the makara. The girls ran off in the direction of the Cavern while Tufan stayed behind, giving an exhausted, panting Makky a brisk rub-down, although he could barely lift his arms himself.

When they reached the cavern, the girls stopped short. A huge boulder blocked the mouth of the cavern. It was far too big and far too heavy for any of them to roll away. If Makky had not been so tired, he might have been able to move it, but he looked close to collapse. They ran back to tell Tufan.

'Uh-oh,' said Tufan, for the third time that octite. 'I think . . . I think I'm going to rain.'

He took a deep breath, and exhaled. A horizontal downpour began, right onto the startled makara. It went on for five whole dinglings.

'Whoohoo!' cheered a relieved Tufan, turning cartwheels on the rocky ground. 'I feel myself again!'

'Tufan!' said Zarpa. 'Stop fooling around and listen! There is a huge boulder across the mouth of the cavern. How are we going to move it?'

'If only Makky wasn't so tired . . .' began Tufan, as he turned to look at the makara.

Then he stopped, his mouth a round O of astonishment. Makky looked completely refreshed, and was leaping around like a little makarakin.

'It was the rain!' cried Zvala happily. Then she made her voice go all low and deep, and announced, as if she was doing the voiceover for a starvision ad. 'Reviving, Rejuvenating Rain—brought to you by Windchild.'

'Hey, you should consider bottling it!' said Zarpa. 'You would make a fortune!'

But Makky was already heading towards the cavern, Tufan behind him. Sometimes, it really seemed as if the creature understood Taratongue!

'Push, Makky, push!' said Tufan urgently.

Using all the legendary makara strength that the Taranauts had only heard about, Makky leaned his mighty head against the boulder, and *pushed*.

The boulder rolled away and landed on its side with a CRASH!

Inside, it was as bright as Taralite. The path that led into the dark inside of the cave was crisscrossed at regular intervals by leaping walls of fire.

'I'll take this,' said Zvala. She closed her eyes and stood very still, imagining a flame in the centre of her forehead and focusing on it. She grew hotter and hotter and redder and redder until she was ready.

Then she simply walked through the walls of fire to the far end of the cavern, picked up the drawstring bag sitting on a low ledge, and walked back to the entrance, getting hotter and hotter along the way.

'Sorry, Zvala, we can't wait for you to cool down,' said Zarpa, 'we have to head back immediately.'

'Don't worry,' Tufan reassured her. 'We're crossing the Laughing Lake again, so I will be able to rain on you and cool you down the moment we reach the other side. Now, are you ready to go?'

Riddle 4

The Taranauts crowded around Zarpa's bed, where Zvala had placed the bag. They had made it to their rooms just five dinglings before Taranite. It was now way past their bedtime, but they were too excited to sleep.

Zarpa opened the bag and upturned it. Onto the bed tumbled a palmyra scroll. Tufan quickly unrolled it.

First in the fourth
And fourth in the first
Find the shapes now
Or be forever curst
If you answer the riddle right
It will vanish out of sight

'It is a Stardoku puzzle!' cried Zvala. She studied it for a while. 'So there are "four basic shapes—circles, triangles, hearts, and stars. And there are four grids of four squares each. Now we have to fill up the squares so that no shape repeats in a row, *or* in a column, *or* in a grid."'

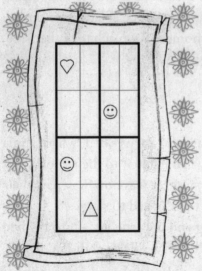

There was complete silence as each of the Taranauts worked on their palmyra sheets.

'Solved it!' yelled Zvala. 'Now what?'

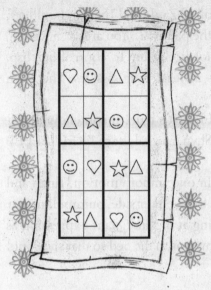

'First in the fourth and fourth in the first . . .' read Zarpa. 'What shape is the first shape in the fourth row? A star! What is the fourth shape in the first row? Also a star!'

'But what if it means column and not row?' said Tufan. 'First shape in the fourth column? Also star! And fourth shape in first column? Star again! It has to be right!'

Zvala frowned. 'So the answer is stars? And what we have finally is . . .'

'MITHYA POSSESSES 0 STARS!' they all chorused.

Suddenly, the room was filled with Shaap Azur's childish giggles. It seemed to come from the palmyra scroll.

'Heeeee heee heeee!' he chortled. 'Heee heeee!'

The Taranauts clutched each other in fear.

Then the voice began to sing tauntingly, 'Mithya possesses *no* stars . . . Mithya possesses *no* stars . . .' There was a pause, and then a flat voice took over. 'This is a pre-recorded message. If you wish to access this message again, please dial 980SHYN&*$.'

The Taranauts heaved a sigh of relief as they watched the star rise from the palmyra and disappear.

Putting her arms around Zvala and Tufan's shoulders, Zarpa shook her fist at the palmyra. 'You are sss*so* wrong, missster!' she hissed, not bothering to control her lisp. 'Mithya now possesses at least four sssstars. The Shyn Emeralds are free!'

'EEEEEEEEEEEEEEE! It's true! It somehow didn't sink in until now! The Shyn Emeralds are FREE! EEEEE . . . . . heyyyyyy!'

But it was too late. In one smooth motion, Tufan and Zarpa jumped on Zvala from either side, pummelling her with pillows and laughing at her indignant expression as they toppled her face down onto the bed so that she could scream no more.

Twelve

Zvala was tossing around on her bed. 'I'm going to stay up all Taranite,' she mumbled sleepily. 'I'm going to stay up until Taralite . . .' She cracked one eye open sleepily. Then she sat bolt upright, threw off the covers and ran to the balcony.

Trizillions of Shynkos were on the street below, bathed in the glorious green light of the Shyn Emeralds, and they were all calling her name. 'ZVA-LA! ZVA-LA! ZVA-LA!'

A huge cheer went up from the crowd as soon as they saw her. People threw her kisses, flowers, and stuffed baloodis, her favourite kind of soft toy. Mithyakins held up placards and posters—'Taranauts—We LOVE You!' 'Zvala—You put the shine back in SHYN' 'Taranauts—The REAL Stars of Mithya!'

Zvala looked up at the Shyn Emeralds, tears pricking the back of her eyes and throat. How she had missed them!

Two pairs of running feet thundered into her room and Zarpa and Tufan burst into the balcony. An even bigger cheer went up from the crowd and a trizillion freezeframes click-clicked madly. The Taranauts grinned and waved and waved and grinned.

Then Zarpa glanced at her dingdial. 'Uffpah! We all completely overslept! It's only ten dinglings to the communication systems coming back,' she said. 'We better get back inside and await orders from Ms Shuk Tee.'

Precisely ten dinglings later, Zarpa's summoner beeped. She turned it on immediately.

Shuk Tee's rich voice filled the room. 'Congratulations, Taranauts! All of you have performed way beyond our expectations and I am proud of you!'

The Taranauts smiled at each other.

'Please report to Kay Laas before Taranite—the Emperaza would like to congratulate you personally, and—' Shuk Tee's voice softened—'it has been a while since I saw Makky.'

There was a pause.

'Oh, and all of you can go home for one octite tomorrow.'

'Let's go!' said Zarpa, throwing her things into her backsack.

'Not so fast! I need a shower first,' said Tufan, ducking into the bathroom with his can of Max Deo before the others could protest.

With Shuk Tee leading the way, the Taranauts marched solemnly into the Throne Room at the Palace, and bowed before the Emperaza. But he was not alone. Around him, on smaller thrones, sat the Marazas and Maranis of all the eight worlds of Mithya. They were all clapping.

'Welcome, Taranauts!' boomed Shoon Ya. 'Welcome, rescuers of the Shyn Emeralds! Mithya is indebted to you. Please, tell us all about it.'

The Taranauts began to speak. After they had finished describing their adventures, they displayed the heavy lexpads they had carried around in Shyn, and described how they had cracked the most important riddle of all—the Riddle of the Shyn Tongues.

'Your Starness,' said Zvala, bowing to the Marani of Shyn. 'The

mithyakos of Shyn have been really foolish. We have fought with each other because of the different languages we speak. It took two outsiders—my fellow Taranauts—to figure out that we all, in fact, speak different versions of exactly the same language, which is Taratongue itself.'

'The Marani of Shyn looked up from the notes she had been furiously scratchscribing. 'First thing in the morning, I will draw up plans for "Learn Taratongue" workshops across Shyn. Then I will send the royal linguists back to school. Dunderheads!'

Tufan snorted.

'Shut up!' hissed Zarpa.

'Marvellous work, Taranauts!' said Shoon Ya. 'I will see you back in Kay Laas one octite from now, when you will return to your coaches and trainers for seven more octites. Then you will decide which Tarasuns you want to rescue next.'

'Eeeeeee!' danced Zvala, the moment they were out of the Throne Room. 'I'm off! I'm off!'

'Me too!' said Zarpa, giving her a hug. 'And I'm going in style! The Marani said I could travel back to Sparkl with her in the royal aqualimo!'

Tufan smiled a small smile. 'Have fun, you guys!' he said, thrusting his hands deep into his pockets and hunching his shoulders. 'I guess I'll just hang around here and explore the Palace. Ms Shuk Tee said I could.'

Zvala stopped dancing. 'Or . . .' she said slowly. 'You could come back with me! Ma loves anyone who can finish three-quarters of a galumpie.'

'You . . . you mean that?' asked Tufan.

'Of course, silly!' said Zvala, taking his arm and propelling him along. 'Now go pack, quickly!'

'Do I have time for a . . .'

'NO!' yelled Zvala.

'Just kidding!' grinned Tufan, as he raced to his room.

Thirteen

'WERE YOU ALL ASLEEP? HOW DARE YOU LET IT HAPPEN?'

Deep in his citadel, Xad Yuntra, somewhere on the Downside, Shaap Azur slammed his fist hard against the wall and glared furiously at his trusted crack team of lieutenants, the fearsome Ograzurs.

'Fools! Three thumb-sized mithyakins have got away with the Shyn Emeralds! Shoon Ya and Shuk Tee must be rolling on the floor, laughing!'

An icy wind swept the room. Unwashed, unkempt, and very, very angry, Shaap Azur had been pacing the room since the Shyn Emeralds had spun out of the Spinternet to their places in the sky above Shyn, glowing and sparkling.

His glacier breath turned the Ograzurs' blood to ice. They shifted from foot to foot, carefully averting their gaze from their master's.

'M-m-master,' one of them stuttered. 'We never imagined that the little brats would even be able to reach the riddles, leave alone solve them. Why, you yourself said . . .'

'Never mind what I said!' hissed Shaap Azur quickly, turning his bloodshot eyes on the Ograzurs. 'What matters is that we are now officially the laughing stock of Mithya—AAAAARRRRRGHHH!' He picked up a chair and flung it against the door. The Ograzurs winced.

'Master,' said one of them finally, raising her head. 'Forgive us. We have let you down.'

'Rest assured, Master,' said another, placing his arm on his head in a solemn vow. 'It will not happen again.

Not one Tarasun shall escape the Spinternet again, not one!'

'Not one!' chorused the Ograzurs, hands on their heads.

'They'd better not,' said Shaap Azur. 'You know what will happen if we fail. It is back to the Fiery Lands for us—this time forever!' The Ograzurs shuddered.

Shaap Azur's face twisted in rage. Throwing his head back and clenching his fists, he sent forth a terrifying warning. Shoon Ya heard it. Shuk Tee heard it. And all the people in the eight worlds of Mithya—seven in still-dark and one lit up again—heard it:

'From this dingling on, Taranauts, I will be watching you! BE-WARE!'

At the Magmalift, the Taranauts looked at each other, a chill running down their spines. Of course they had rescued the Shyn Emeralds and they had every reason to be proud, but now that Shaap Azur was on the alert, would they *ever* be able to rescue even *one* of the other 28 Tarasuns?